MISSION DRIVEN
LA AVISPA

STANLEY FORD

MISSION DRIVEN
LA AVISPA

This is a work of fiction. All of the characters, names, incidents, organizations, and dialogue in this novel are either the products of the author's imagination or are used fictitiously.

iUniverse books may be ordered through booksellers or by contacting:

iUniverse
1663 Liberty Drive
Bloomington, IN 47403
www.iuniverse.com
844-349-9409

ISBN: 978-1-6632-4288-4 (sc)
ISBN: 978-1-6632-4287-7 (e)

Library of Congress Control Number: 2022914132

Print information available on the last page.

iUniverse rev. date: 07/29/2022

ACKNOWLEDGEMENT

LIZANNA SVENDESEN (For her inspiration and support)

KAREN WHITTAKER – (for her encouragement and assistance)

PROLOGUE

Shortly after, she saw the Santa Lucia making its way majestically out of the harbor. It was such a pity; she was a beautiful boat. With that Juanita waited a while longer until it had cleared the other boats and the entrance to the harbor then she remotely triggered the bomb. There was a brilliant flash then the accompanying sound of a massive explosion. There was debris and a smoldering fire for a while and then just driftwood. By the time the fireboat and the police arrived there was hardly anything to see.

Juanita made her way down from the lookout and got a taxi back to the hotel where she checked out and headed to the airport for a flight by commuter aircraft to Dominica Republic and the first leg on her journey back home.

CHAPTER 1

The meeting was set for 1500hours, but Juanita arrived at the location at 1430hours to have a look around and refresh herself with the layout of the area. The area, known as Robins Bay in the parish of St. Mary, was known to her as she had been there several times before, mostly to attend birthday functions put on by friends of Kareem. The actual venue for the meeting was a rustic little restaurant on a cliff above the sea. Robins Bay itself had somewhat of a reputation as it was rumored that in the late sixties to early seventies it was a major pick-up point for marijuana being shipped out of the island. Those rumors were not very farfetched either as during that period the area had become somewhat of a Hippie colony with many Americans who were caught up in that culture in the United States expanding their quest for the lifestyle to Jamaica. And what better venue could they ask for. It was rural but still near enough to shopping areas, it had a beach, luxurious tropical climate, and an abundance of sunshine. At present the area has become a quiet little village where the folks are involved mostly in fishing and entertaining the few tourists who visit.

Having looked around the property Juanita entered and sat by a table where she had a view of the narrow road leading to the restaurant. She ordered a cold Red Stripe beer and began studying the menu. At 1455hours she saw a black Range Rover approaching and instantly recognized it as that driven by Tom Baptist her contact.

As soon as Tom entered the restaurant and headed towards her Juanita got up and directed him over to another table further back in the dining area. Before sitting they shook hands and he saw to it that she was seated. Tom was of average height with intelligent looking eyes and square shoulders befitting of a football player.

Tom told her that it was his first visit to the restaurant but that he had heard of it and that the food was good. A server came over and further banter was halted as they turned their attention to ordering their meal.

During the meal they shared stories about their experiences and travels around the island. When next Tom spoke, he was direct and businesslike.

"Juanita" he said, "or should I say La Avispa?" Juanita was caught off guard but as she pushed back on the table he quickly countered, "Relax Juanita we are friends here." "Are we Tom?" "Please explain."

"Juanita I will get directly to the point." "Please do Tom I am all ears."

"I know you have seen me around on a number of occasions in the company of your friend Kareem from the Jamaican military and in functions put on by staff members of the US Embassy."

"What you don't know about me is what I do." "That I will soon explain."

"But let me tell you a little more about you before I do that."

"You were born in the Dominican Republic but moved to the USA to attend college." "Instead of attending college, however, you enlisted in the US Marines."

"While in training your parents were killed in a boat explosion orchestrated by a Mexican cartel. Although your parents were not the actual targets their death had such profound impact on you that you decided to take on the cartels and fight them from within."

"I will not prolong your curiosity any longer. La Avispa we have been tracking you for some time from you were in the cartel."

"I am with the DEA, and we had an agent embedded covertly with the cartel you were with."

"He was very impressed by you and always knew there was something different about you, you were just not an ordinary cartel criminal or killer."

"You were mission driven." "And so, he wanted to find out what was your mission."

"For that reason, he stuck very close to you and would always volunteer to go with you on some of your errands or reconnaissance."

"Yes, Juanita I am with the DEA, and I want you to come work with us on an upcoming mission, one that we think would give you great satisfaction."

After outlining the general details of the mission Tom told her he would give her forty-eight hours to think it over and get back to him with her answer.

Whether it was the fact that she was finding life getting a bit too routine or just the thought of getting back into action against the cartels but within twenty-four hours she contacted Tom and another meeting was set to firm up the arrangements.

CHAPTER 2

The helicopter took off at 2100hours from a small airport just outside the city of McAllen, Texas, and flew low over the border into Mexican territory. The trip lasted about one hour and then it dropped suddenly and hovered for a few seconds before landing in a small clearing surrounded by trees and complete darkness. The copilot pointed Juanita toward a barely visible light flickering in the darkness. As soon as she acknowledged seeing the light the door was opened and she was out and moving towards it, with the voice of the copilot ringing in her ears. "Remember be back here tomorrow at 0300hours or you will have a long walk back home." The minute she was clear of the helicopter it was off. She walked tentatively towards the light feeling naked and alone.

On closing on the light, she uttered the words, "Beautiful weather." Then from behind the light came the response. "For cats only." "Hi, Carmen, I am Max."

Carmen was the name she had chosen for the mission, and she suspected that Max was not Max either, but she did not care less. If he worked with her, all would be well. Cross her and he dies.

"Nice meeting you Max." "You have something for me I think." "Yes, here it is and let us get going."

Max handed Juanita a Glock 17 complete with silencer and two extra magazines then they headed off on a narrow track through the woods. Max was a small bodied furtive looking individual with a restless bounding walk even in the dark.

After about ten minutes brisk walking they came to a small truck cleverly hidden in the woods at the end of a dirt road.

They traveled for about two and a half hours before Max turned off onto an even narrower road that appeared to be leading nowhere. In the end it brought them to a small house neatly tucked into a strand of trees. Despite being so remote it could be seen, even in the dark, that it was well kept. Juanita thanked Max and reminded him to come to collect her at 0800hours the next morning. Max acknowledged and left.

As soon as Max was out of sight Juanita cautiously entered the house, spent a short while inside then slipped out through a side door and disappeared into the woods. She found what looked like a good spot where she would be comfortable and be able to see the cottage. She opened her knapsack and took out an old military style jacket that would be exactly right for her comfort during the night. She had no intention of sleeping in the house.

When Max arrived the next morning Juanita was wearing a head scarf and dressed as a rural Mexican female. Max spluttered. "Is that you Carmen?" "In live and living colors Max." "We have places to go and work to do."

Juanita's plan was to do a detailed reconnaissance of the areas of interest and the location of her intended target as per her briefing. Most important she had to plan her strategy, her attack plan and escape routes. She would leave nothing up to chance and so must plan contingencies. To achieve all that she asked Max to drop her at a midway point and to return in two hours.

Mendez in the state of Tamaulipas is an exceedingly small town, with a population of about nine hundred. The people were friendly, so she made small talk and asked innocent sounding questions as she moved around. At one point she stopped and had a meal of tacos and tamales with fruit juice. She even had some attractively packaged for her to take home.

Max was right on time as she finished her wondering around. It was now time to head back to the cabin where she would put all the pieces of her plan together before night.

Her mission as was outlined by Tom was straightforward. She was to terminate the leader of a cartel that has been operating in the neighboring region of Matamoros.

As part of her briefing Tom had outlined to her the background on what was happening and why the mission was critical. In doing so he had hoped to tap into her strong repulsion for the cartels and to paint a picture she would find hard to turn down.

Tom outlined it this way.

Angelo Palomino is the leader of "La familia Nueva," (the new family) cartel and the mastermind behind assaults on the drug rehabilitation centers known as annexes, operating from Mendez to as far as Ciudad Juarez (Juarez City)

Along with his cartel Angelo moved into the void created by lack of state control of the rehabilitation centers and has become the main perpetrator of something that was started by the Familia Michoacana cartel. It was that cartel that began the employment of addicts at the rehabilitation centers to do their illegal activities.

The criminal organizations use the centers to recruit "halcones" as they are referred to, who function as lookouts, hitmen, and drug dealers and to 'disappear' people.

The matter has been overlooked for years by the authorities, from the state and municipal level to the federal authorities who see it as an unnecessary expenditure and a distraction from their agenda. All this neglect comes against the backdrop of a skyrocketing consumption of drugs ranging from marihuana to methamphetamines.

With the lack of interest on the part of the government private individuals took it upon themselves to set up rehabilitation centers with their own capital.

Unfortunately, while the government turned its back on the existence of the centers the criminal groups did not and move in to exploit them. They started off by charging rental fees or protection money then gradually begin to engage in more miscreant actions and eventual recruitment. While this takes place the operators of the center will have to comply with the demands or face severe repercussions and death. In the end they are simply spectators looking on while the criminal gangs use the annexes to expand their illicit businesses. It was not long however, that rivalry developed between different gangs over the control of the centers. This lead at timed to bloody clashes and abductions of the residents of the centers, some of whom were forced into working for the cartels or were murdered.

After one such attack Juan Martinez the operator of the Angel's Nest center decided he had had enough and would do something about it. Assessing the risk involved Juan approached Alberto Llamas the governor of Tamaulipas with his plan. He had known the governor since childhood days and had much confidence in him. The governor was very receptive to the plan and assured his assistance. It was no secret that the governor had become disillusioned by the lack of support by the federal government and was quite unhappy with the increasing criminal activities in the region. He felt that an example must be set before the already unpleasant situation spread over the entire country.

The plan outlined was that Governor Llamas would contact his trusted friend Miguel Lopez the governor of Nuevo Leon. Lopez was unique in that he was an independently elected governor not connected to a political party and he had vowed from inception to fight crime in all form in his region. This made him a very brave but respected individual by the United States law enforcement entities in Mexico. Governor Lopez would seek the assistance of the United States DEA in getting rid of Angelo Palomino. It was surmised that by having outside help it would lessen the chance of repercussions and a major war between the various criminal groups.

Governor Lopez assured his friend Governor Llamas that he would make the necessary arrangements and get things moving as quickly as possible.

True to his word Governor Lopez contacted the DEA office in Texas and outlined the plan. The DEA who had been monitoring the situation for some time along with the Bureau of Alcohol Tobacco and Firearms (ATF) could hardly believe this good fortune and immediately started planning.

Angelo Palomino's house was a short distance out of the town. Except for a very imposing gate and a high wall at the front the rest of the property was surrounded by a chain link metal fence topped with razor wire. The compound was well lit, but it was near to a thick wood that extended for quite a distance on both sides and to the rear.

Juanita (Carmen) got out of the vehicle about a half mile from the house and headed into the woods. She had to be at the rear fence by 1950 hours.

Max was instructed to return for her at the same point he dropped her at precisely 2220 Hours.

On reaching the fence Juanita immediately got to work cutting a hole in the fence. She followed the precise protocol she had learnt in the military, cut from the bottom and for just as high as is necessary.

Everything was going to plan so far, so she waited to make her next move.

Angelo was a creature of habit, not a good trait for someone engaged in his type of activities. Every night he would go by the pool at precisely 2215hours, have one glass of scotch then swim until 2300hours. While he is swimming there would be one guard at the front of the house and one patrolling the compound. Then at 2300hours an additional guard would assume duty at the rear of the building, near the pool.

Juanita waited patiently in the woods by the breach she had made in the fence.

At precisely 2200Hours there was a power cut in the area, compliment of the DEA and contacts within the energy company.

Juanita now had thirty seconds to complete her mission before the standby generator kicked in.

As the lights went out, she was through the fence and at the poolside in less than 10 seconds. She headed directly for Angelo and fired twice, once in the head and the other to the chest. She was turning to leave when she saw the guard coming around the side of the building, he was in the process of raising his AK 47 rifle when she fired two rounds into his chest. He doubled over and went down with his weapon making a clattering sound on the concrete. She dashed for the fence, and she was hardly through when the lights from the generator came on.

She moved as quickly as her skills would allow her through the trees to be at the pickup point for Max to collect her.

She got to the area and took cover behind a large tree by the road. She was there for about three minutes when she heard the motorcycle approaching. Through the ambient light she could make out a rider and a pillion. As they approached her something must have caught their attention as they slowed, and the pillion fired a few rounds into the tree line. Juanita was certain they were not firing at her but nevertheless she was taking no chances. As soon as they got abreast of her, she fired on them, the cycle went down with a crash taking both persons. She broke cover and shot them both. Just as she pondered her next move, she heard the familiar sound of Max's truck approaching from the opposite direction. She got in the vehicle, and they headed for the helicopter pick up point.

Max dropped her off and left the area. She was alone with only her pistol, a small light, and a bottle of water compliment of Max.

She melted as much as possible into the trees and waited. The helicopter came into the hover at precisely 0259 Hours and as soon as it was on the ground, she flashed her light three times. On receiving the return signal of two red filtered flashes she sprinted towards the helicopter and was on her way.

They flew in silence back to the drop off point in Texas and from there she was whisked away in a heavily tinted SUV.

CHAPTER 3

Juanita was happy to be back home and enjoying the quiet and easy-going life once more. She sat on the back deck of her cottage overlooking the shimmering blue water of the Caribbean Sea just meters below and stretching for as far as the eyes could see.

She began to reminisce on the trip back home from her mission. She could not help but smile when she remembered her first conversation with Tom. "Juanita, I sent you on a mission to eliminate one target and you reduced the population of a small town." "Do you know what the population of that town was and what it is now"? Before she could answer he laughed and remarked. "I must really factor in significant collateral damage next time." Juanita had mulled on his words, next time.

In reflecting on the trip home, she remembered being driven to El Paso Intelligence Center (EPIC) compound where she was debriefed then driven to the airport. She boarded a Cessna Citation jet and was soon airborne and headed for Ian Fleming airport in Jamaica. Although the aircraft had a capacity of nine passengers there were only three others and herself onboard. The aircraft itself was owned by a large Texas oil company but had been chartered for the trip. That was something Juanita had insisted on, that if she was to be flown into the Ian Fleming airport, she did not want to arrive in a US Government aircraft as she lived just across the road from the airport and the community was a small one. She did not want some curious soul to make the connection.

Her mind had just begun to drift again as she started to contemplate working on other similar missions.

Her reminiscing was cut short as Kareem called to her from inside the cottage. "Honey! How would you like to go deer hunting this weekend?"

"What are you talking about, there are not deer in Jamaica."

"Oh yes there is there are whitetail deer and two of my friends have invited us to join them on Saturday."

"I didn't know that."

"Yes, they were being kept in a private zoo as tourist attraction in Portland but when Hurricane Gilbert hit the island in 1988 six of them escaped and they started breeding quickly and soon became a major nuisance for the farmers."

"Ok, and is hunting them legal"?

"Yes, as long as it is not done in forest reserves, game reserves and national parks."

"Very interesting, but why do you think I would want to shoot those innocent looking animals."

"Ah! It will be fun, don't be a spoil sport."

"Ok boss, I will go."

"Don't give me any of that boss stuff." "Come here, give me a hug my little sugar plumb."

"Oh, brother you are really on a roll."

"So, who are these friends we are going with"?

"You know Tom from the US Embassy and Gairy the manager of the garage in Ocho Rios where we service our vehicles."

"Yes, I know them."

On the mention of Tom's name Juanita suddenly felt a tinge of guilt and a realization that something had to be done to preserve her relationship with Kareem while not jeopardizing her ability to act on potential missions.

She had been giving Kareem bits and pieces about her and her former life, but he did not know the half and she was worried about his reaction if he found out.

On the last mission she had simply told him that because of her fluency in Spanish and being a native of the Dominican Republic Tom had asked her to function as a third party in the interviewing of a Dominican national in Texas.

Juanita decided that she had to manage the present situation with alacrity before it spiraled out of control. First, she had to get to Tom and let him know that under no circumstance he should disclose anything about her past to Kareem. She also planned to tell him that she does not want to be involved in any other missions such as the last one. She wanted to be the person being in charge in the pursuit of her missions towards her objective and did not want to be distracted. With that in mind, however, she still thought it would be prudent to keep Tom on her side just in case she might need his assistance.

Secondly, she will tell Kareem that due to the last job she did the door was opened for other such opportunities to work with the Embassy throughout Latin America and the Caribbean region.

She felt that once these two bases were covered it would be less problematic and unnecessary to explain every time she wanted to travel. And she might be travelling quite often.

The day of the hunt came and went and was quite successful and at the end the team headed to Gairy's home in Ocho Rios. The hunt had gotten two young bucks. Throughout the trip back from the field and at the home it was noticed that Juanita had become quite taciturn and somber even when jokes were being poked at her. They also made much about how she had dropped the first deer with a brilliant shot to the head from fifty meters away and barely visible through the trees. She just shrugged it off and said it was thanks to her brothers who had taught her to shoot rabbits in her childhood days back in the Dominican Republic.

On their return to the cottage that evening Juanita and Kareem had dinner then went to sit on the back deck to relax and have a drink.

She seized upon the moment to tell Kareem that while they were on the hunt Tom had called her aside and had told her that based on the last job, he had a proposal for her to work for the Embassy.

That of course was not true. It was she who had pulled Tom aside to lay out her plans. She explained to Tom that based on the last mission and what she had seen she was thinking of making some visits back to the region. She then explained that Kareem was under no circumstance to know what she was up to and to that extent she was asking him, Tom, to provide cover for her by pretending that she was collaborating with him while not exactly doing so. That, she explained would be their only level of involvement as she did not want to be tied directly to him or the agency so their credibility would not be jeopardized in the case of any unforeseen event.

Tom had listened carefully to her proposal and gave his approval if she in return would keep the arrangement just between, herself, him, and Kareem.

Both agreed, and they rejoined the hunting party.

"Is that why you were so quiet on the way back"? "I guess you were giving it much thought."

"Yes, I was."

"So, what did you decide"?

"I am thinking about taking it, but I wanted to get your opinion and consent."

"Well honey I think that is a good opportunity, I think you should take it by all means."

"Afterall, I see how restless you seem to get sometimes." "It would definitely be something else to keep you going along with the boat business."

"Thank you so much honey, you are knowing me so well."

"Ok any idea how soon you might be required"?

"No not yet but Tom will be my contact and will let me know."

"Hopefully, it will not be too long".

"Oh! My goodness are you getting tired of me"?

"Never my love."

Juanita was keeping her cards close to her chest and preparing herself mentally for what might be ahead.

She realized that the deception of Kareem was a high price to pay for their relationship should he ever become aware of her identity and what she was really involved with, but she was prepared to take the chance in pursuance of her sworn mission to fight the Mexican cartels.

Kareem had become an integral part of her life and at one point she had even wondered if she would go back to that former lifestyle, but the pull was too great and the last mission for Tom had rekindled the flame all over.

With Kareem she had felt at ease and relaxed, even too relaxed. Kareem was a well-trained military officer; he was well educated and in excellent physical shape even at one point trying out for the Jamaica Bob Sledge team but gave it up to concentrate on making the national shooting team instead. He was deeply in love with Juanita seized every opportunity to be with her. Kareem had shown her around the island and had taught her the culture of the people. They went to functions where she met folks from all strata of the society and mingled with foreign dignitaries. She was having a good life but there was still an emptiness. She had to continue her crusade, she was truly mission driven and there was no way of escaping it until she was completely satisfied that she had been effective in the fight against the evils of the cartels.

CHAPTER 4

Juanita arrived in St. Johns, Antigua, from Jamaica late Sunday afternoon. She checked into the Starfish Halcyon Cove hotel and planned to be there for two days.

That same night she met with Jose Vargas who had flown in from Mexico by way of Miami. The meeting was held on the beach, away from the relatively full hotel with all its guests milling around, each in their own world filled with the euphoria often generated by a leisurely life at a hotel teeming with vacationers.

Jose Vargas was to be her facilitator in Mexico when she arrived there. He would make all plans for her and become her invisible shadow and facilitator. After the meeting they would not meet again unless necessary. Jose had collaborated with her before as a member of her three-man team but this time they would be working without the cleaner, the third member of the team. If it became necessary Jose would fill that role.

Jose left immediately following the meeting and flew out that same night.

On checking out Juanita headed for Dominica Republic where she spent three days. While in Dominica Republic she visited several relatives, old family friends and her parent and siblings' grave sites. She also had time to relive the changes in her life. Juanita reflected on what had gotten her to this place in her and were might it lead. She vividly remembers her days in training as a United States

Marine and how she was selected for sniper training because of her competence in shooting. She remembered well how she loved shooting and enjoyed her chosen field. Then she remembered the day she got the tragic news that her family had been killed by members of a drug cartel and the vow she had made to avenge their deaths by fighting the cartels. It did not matter to her that their deaths were due to mistaken identity they could sort out that mistake when they met their maker in the other life. She remembered leaving the Marines and returning to the Dominican Republic where she remained for three years. While there she settled family business and then went into an intensive training program to prepare her for what was ahead. She joined the shooting club and entered just about every shooting competition that came her way. Along with her shooting she got involved in the martial arts and an overall intense fitness program. Following all that training she left her country for Mexico where she eventually found her way into a small drug gang. That gang became her steppingstone to her ultimate goal which was to get into a cartel. Once there and being accepted with her skills she figured she would be able to do maximum damage or die trying. After cooperating with the cartel she decided to be a free agent who would be paid for carrying out jobs on its behalf. Under normal circumstances she would have been eliminated, but she had gained such respect that they allowed her to have her way. That would be a tragic mistake for them in the end. They had made her into what she had become, and they would reap the whirlwind they had created.

On the last evening before departing the Dominican Republic Juanita decided to go by the beach for a long walk and to reflect. She was almost at the end of her walk and the shades of night were closing in, so she began to hasten her steps. As she did, she noticed a young man coming towards her. When he came alongside, he greeted her and asked. "Are you from around here?"

"Why do you ask?" Replied Juanita.

"Just curious as I have never seen you around before."

"Ok, well no I am not I am a visitor."

"You are very pretty."

"Thank you, and you are very kind."

"Would you like me to tag along with you and show you around?"

"Thanks for the offer but I must be going."

"Ok, in that case can I sell you something that will make you feel really good?"

"What are you talking about?"

"I have some really good weed, you know marijuana."

"No thanks I don't do that rubbish."

"But this is good stuff, it's from St. Vincent."

"No thanks and I think you had better be going."

"Don't be like that, I thought you were cool, but I guess not."

"Yes, you got that right, I am not cool when it comes to doing drugs."

"Ok, to each his own." Then suddenly he grabbed her hand and whispered to her come with me. Juanita very out of character found herself running with him towards a grove of trees. Her first instinct would have been to lash out at him on being grabbed but something told her not to. Maybe it was his demeanor, despite being a drug pusher and his polite manner that saved him. Once in the trees he whispered to her to be quiet, then he explained. "I am not really a drug pusher and I know you don't do drugs." "I am actually an old friend of your family through your late brother, but you would not remember me."

"Would you by any chance be Dominic Rios?"

"Wow! You have quite a memory, yes, I am."

"I thought you looked familiar and that might have been what saved you from an ass whipping tonight when you grabbed me." Dominic laughed quietly and Juanita broke into a smile.

"Could you really do that, I mean whip me."

"I probably could." "So anyway, why were you out here?"

Dominic explained to Juanita that there is a group of drug dealers that harass persons on the beach at nights and especially young unsuspecting females. These unsuspecting females are told about them, and some come to buy drugs and end up getting more than they bargained for, in that they are not only drugged but end up being sexually molested. Juanita's curiosity was aroused. "So, are they around tonight?"

"Yes, they are that is why I took you out of harm's way."

"Where are they now?"

"They are just a short distance down the beach, heading this way."

"There are three of them tonight."

"Do you want to take them in?" "If you do, I will help you."

"Sure, but I don't want to endanger you."

"I will be fine just let me know what you want me to do."

Dominic explained that she should let them approach her and offer to sell her drugs. Once she is in possession of the drugs, she should hold it up as if to inspect it. That would be his signal to move in.

Juanita made Dominic promise her one thing and that was not to expose her identity. The story would be that he saw the tourist about to be mugged by the group and he moved in. A scuffle ensued and he with the assistance of the tourist got the better of them. The tourist, however, did not want to be involved and left the scene immediately after the incident. Dominic agreed.

As they saw the three men approaching in the distance Juanita ambled out onto the narrow pathway running along the seashore.

When they reached her one member of the group immediately declared that they had what she wanted.

"And what would that be that you think I want?" "And who are you guys anyway?"

"We are they guys that are going to give you an enjoyable time tonight."

"Really, and how are you planning to do that?"

"Ok, too much argument let's start with this then we can take it from there."

"Start with what?"

"The good stuff baby."

"Do you mean drugs?"

"Yes, baby what else."

"So where is the stuff?"

"Yes, baby here it is." "First this then this." And with that he was handing her the drugs while his cronies were holding on to the front of their pants in a suggestive manner.

Juanita reached out for the drugs and held it up, but at the same instance she delivered a withering kick into the groin of the one who was directly in front of her. As he doubled over, she delivered another kick to the head that sent him flat on his back. The other man to her left pulled out a knife and lunged towards her. She side stepped and grabbed his arm while pulling him forward with her left arm. This put her in the right position to smash his nose with the heel of her hand. With the knife now out of his hand she delivered a devastating kick to the chest that had him stumbling backways before hitting the ground. By then Dominic had arrived and was cuffing the third man who seemed to be in a state of shock. He looked wide eyed at Juanita and beckoned her to go. Then he signaled her to call him later. While waiting on the men earlier he had given her his number. It was a good thing.

In a few minutes, a police vehicle arrived, and the men were taken away.

When Juanita called later that night, they had a short conversation and she promised to keep in touch with him. She could sense that he was still in a state of shock at what he had seen.

Having made herself visible in the country and reaffirming her vow to avenge her family she flew out to Mexico to the fate that awaited her and anyone who she targeted.

On arrival in Nuevo Leon, she headed for the Krystal hotel where reservation had been made.

With constant pressure on Mexico both internally and externally and culminating in the arrest or imprisonment of some top cartel leaders the country's criminal landscape began to be fragmented.

That forced the traditional cartels to change their normal posture, they gave way to smaller cartels which unfortunately quickly grew to become replicas of the ones they took over from.

All the new Cartels like their predecessors seem to have learnt from Colombia's Cali Cartel that to survive they had to have a strong leader and must establish connections to Mexico's political and economic elite. To that end they successfully penetrated government and security forces wherever they operate. It was a case of offering bribes rather than enduring constant harassment.

Ramon Mendoza had set up camp in Tijuana and established what became known as the New Tijuana Cartel.

He would be the first of the new cartel leaders to be target by Juanita.

Her thinking was strategic Ramon had recently negotiated a pact with Noa Gonzales the leader of the Brotherhood Cartel, operating out of Culiacan, Sinaloa. She figured that by eliminating Ramon, Noa would move quickly to further unite both cartels and become the overall boss.

Juanita had been bidding her time awaiting the ideal opportunity to make her move. She now got information that put her schedule on a fast track to spring into action. It was time to pay a visit to Tijuana and by extension Ramon Mendoza. For this mission Jose would precede her to make the necessary arrangements.

Although Juanita had heard much about Tijuana she was awestruck by its size and diversity. For a short while when on her way to the hotel she felt overwhelmed. She must have thought this is vastly different from my tiny town of a few thousands on the north coast of Jamaica.

Tijuana city is in Baja California, Mexico, it is often referred to as TJ. by persons from the region. It is the 2nd-largest city in Mexico. It is a large manufacturing and migration center and is well steeped in culture, art, and politics. Tijuana is currently one of the fastest-growing metropolitan areas in Mexico. In September 2019, the city had a population of 1,810,645.

Contributing to this rapid growth in population is its heave involvement in manufacturing and tourism. In the early 21st century, Tijuana became the medical-device manufacturing capital of North America. It is also a growing cultural center and the city is the most visited border city in the world; sharing a border of about 24 km (15 mi) with its sister city San Diego. More than fifty million people cross the border between these two cities every year.

Tijuana traces its modern history to the arrival of Spanish explorers in the 16th century who were mapping the coast of the California. The city was founded on July 11, 1889, when urban development began.

From the founding of the city in 1889 Tijuana saw its future in tourism and from the late 19th century to the first few decades of the 20th century, the city attracted large numbers of visitors.

Legal drinking and gambling attracted U.S nationals in the 1920s during Prohibition. This led to the area of the Avenue of the Revolution becoming the tourist center, with casinos and hotels and the birthplace of the now famous Caesar salad.

Following the attack on the on 9/11 in the United States and an escalation in drug crimes border control was made much tighter and this resulted in a decline in tourism.

The decline gradually waned and in recent years, the city has become an important city of commerce and migration for Mexico and US. In addition to tourists from the US it now receives many tourists from, China, Japan, and the south of Mexico. Through the revitalization of cultural and business festivals, the city has improved its image before the world and now stands out as a competitive city for investment. Entwined with its growth and achievements was a dangerous subculture of drug and drug related violence, including human trafficking. This has put tremendous strain on the government system at all levels.

A new colonel had been assigned to the Tijuana area as the military commander for the region. It had by now become standard practice for the cartels to embrace the police and military units operating in their areas. It was by no means strange, therefore, when Ramon Mendoza decided to lay on a lavish feast for the new Colonel. It would give him the opportunity to assess the new officer and form his opinion of him to determine how he operate going forward. It was also an excellent opportunity for him to impress on the Colonel how much control he had in the region to the extent he could organize such a function and have in attendance persons from the top echelon of the area down to the ordinary man on the street. That, he was sure must go a long way to impress his main guest.

The function was held at a relatively new hotel just outside the city limit, in what was a rather pastoral setting, with cool climate, lush green grass and a canopy of stars not defused by the brilliant lights of the city.

What Ramon did not bargain on however was the fact that in the crowd, all dressed like she was stepping off the front cover of a fashion magazine, was someone who had vowed to speed his exit from this world and into the next. Juanita was standing there all elegantly dressed in a clinging red dress like a seductive siren bidding her time to move in and ensnare her target.

Juanita had arrived in Tijuana two days before the event was to be held and once checked into the hotel, she spent almost her entire time away from it and out on the street. She toured the city extensively gathering as much information as possible. She wanted to feel the pulse of the city while staying as low-keyed as possible. The few places of interest that are normally frequented by tourists that she decided to visit were places that would in their own way provide her with information she sought to acquire while still maintaining her anonymity. To that end she visited the Avenue of the Revolution which was the first road in Tijuana to be paved, it was from its earliest days a popular destination for American tourists who crossed the border from California and it has remained so.

Other places visited were the Tijuana Cultural Center, the busy Hidalgo open-air market with its considerable number of stalls selling a variety of products and the Santa Cecilia Plaza where she was drawn in by its lively music.

Time went by quickly and the night of the function had arrived. Juanita was as ready as she could be, she was about to live up to the reputation that had acquired her the name La Avispa, the wasp.

The Colonel gave a short speech in which he stressed the fact that he was impressed by what he had seen and the orderliness of the function. He did say, however, "I have been in the military for a long time, I have seen a lot and I know that not all the time things are the way they appear on the surface." "Rest assured that I will not be duped, I am responsible for the security and overall safety of the area and no one else." "Life here will be a partnership between my command and you the good folks of the area." "We respect each other, and we get along, step out of line and there will be consequences."

The crowd received the address with mixed feelings, no doubt they had heard similar ones before. Some in the crowd looked on with blank stares, some with smirks and others just shook their heads.

Immediately after his speech a light rain began, and the Colonel waved to the crowd, smiled, and said that the rain was his signal to head back into the town as he had an important meeting early next morning and he had to go prepare for it.

Ramon thanked the colonel for coming and assured him that he has everything under control and there will be no need for concern.

After the colonel departed most of the crowd drifted away leaving only about thirty well-dressed persons who were special guests. It was to this group that Juanita attached herself and followed it into the hotel.

It was not long before one of Ramon's bodyguards approached her and enquired who she was and if she was a guest of his boss. Juanita was forthright. "Actually, my good man I am new in your area, and I heard about this function, I also heard that your boss is an authority on horses, so I came to meet him and to have an intellectual discussion with him about such." "As you can see, I went and got all dolled up to meet him so I am sure you will not deny me the pleasure." "Come, come don't be shy, close your mouth and let's go."

Juanita was as beautiful as she was confident and forthright. In doing her due diligence She had uncovered Ramon's deep interest in horses and that would be her trump card. Once she had discovered his weakness, her next move had been to research all she could find on horses to fire the opening salvo to gain his attention and then engage him in meaningful conversation. In doing her research, however, Juanita decided to confine her interest to Argentinian horses, that way she would not overextend herself and run the risk of showing her lack of overall knowledge in the subject. She felt it would be much better to maintain her focus on that breed of horse rather than trying to be an expert on all types and breeds.

Juanita is presented to Ramon, and he is visibly impressed. He compliments her on her skin tone and how flawless it is. "Is there a special secret formula that you will keep so close to your chest that you will not even share with a weather-beaten old man"?

"I could but if I did, I would have to kill you."

"Caramba! You didn't just say that." He then let out a mighty roar of laughter.

"I like you, come let's sit I understand you want to talk about my pet subject, horses."

"Yes, I would love that, nothing like learning from the master."

"You flatter me my darling." "But I love it." Another roar of laughter.

"So, my darling Carmen." "Carmen isn't it"?

"Yes, Carmen it is" Juanita had switched back to using the name Carmen.

"How long will you be here in Tijuana"?

"Unfortunately, I fly out first thing tomorrow, have business in Mexico City."

"That's a pity I was just thinking of showing off our beautiful city to you and possibly go horse riding." "Aah well, maybe next time."

"Yes, next time." "Have been here for three days and I must say it has been quite pleasant so I think I will definitely be back."

"So, my good weather-beaten old man would you like to join me in my room for a night cap before I turn into a pumpkin or maybe a horse."

"A spritely little filly might be interesting indeed."

"You are reading my mind; have you been doing much riding recently?" She puts her finger to her mouth. "Don't answer that."

On reaching the room she reaches for a bottle of scotch, having noticed that is what he had been drinking. She handed it to him.

"Please pour a drink for yourself and one for me also, I will only be a minute." With that she disappeared into the bathroom.

When she got back, they toasted each other and started sipping their drinks while still making small talk.

"Are you okay?" "You look a bit tense, take off your jacket and loosen that tie." "That's better."

She than took his glass and took the bottle to pour another drink. "This is your last, we have riding to do, remember."

As she poured the drink, she discretely dropped the powerful drug in it and allowed it to dissolve before handing it to him.

"Wow! I could really get use to this."

"Don't try to impress me old man I'm sure you are not short of such treatment." "If I didn't think so I would not have invited you to my room, I like class."

By the time she had ended the sentence he had fallen flat on his back. She retrieved the old ceremonial dagger she had in the sheath strapped to her inner thigh and plunged it into his chest.

With that done she went to the bathroom and changed her red dress for a simple nurse's uniform, she tied the little red dress around her waist under the uniform, then changed her shoes to make herself look at least three inches shorter than before. Now with pistol in hand she opened the door, as the bodyguard saw her, she fired and caught him before he hit the floor. She pulled him inside, locked the door and hung the do not disturb sign on it then headed for the service elevator.

She exits the hotel at the rear and headed onto the narrow treelined road heading into the nearby village. The plan was to go to a small house along the road and there get rid of the uniform while she waits for Jose.

As she approached the house, she saw two men roughly pushing a young girl to get her inside. They were both armed with pistols.

As luck would have had it the house turned out to be one of the cartel's houses where they held young people they had abducted until they were collected.

One of the men was standing at the door lighting a cigarette while the other pushed the girl inside, his intention was quite clear as he ripped off her clothe as soon as she got through the door.

Juanita had to move fast. She got into the tree line and circled to the rear of the house. When she emerged around the corner to the front of the house, she fell the man at the door with two well placed bullets and in one action entered the door just as the second thug was loosening his belt, with the girl cowering on the table. He turned just in time to see the muzzle flash that would be his bright light that would usher him into the other world.

Juanita quickly took off the uniform, put it on the girl, and told her to run as fast as she could away from there. Then just as she turned to go, she heard the sound of the motorcycle, and something caught her eyes at the same moment the young girl shouted to her. She was just able to push the girl out of the way while dropping to the floor herself. The house was suddenly being peppered with bullets as the two assailants dismounted the cycle and opened fire with handguns. Juanita knew she was in a bad place and to get out she would have to think fast if she was going to get out alive. From her position on the floor, she shot out the light then kicked the table over and pushed it up to the door. Her next move was quite unexpected even for the girl. Juanita shouted to the two men to come for the girl if they wanted her, she said there was no need for anyone got hurt. The men seemed to have been caught off guard by this move and hesitated even as Juanita yanked the girl to her feet, pushed her in front of her and threw out her pistol the men visibly relaxed, big mistake. From under the arm of the girl Juanita shot both men, then pushing the girl aside she dove behind the table and proceeded to finish them off. Satisfied that they were no longer a threat she took the girl by the hand and ran out of the house and into the woods, just stopping long enough to retrieve her Glock. The pistol from one of the men she had shot earlier had come in handy just at the right time.

When they were in the woods awaiting the arrival of Jose the girl told her that her name was Anita and that the men had taken her away from a drug rehabilitation center along with two other children. Anita said there were six men in all but four of them had stopped by a shop along the road with the other two other girls. Anita said they were drinking heavily, and she decided to make a run for it into the woods. She said they tried to come after her, but she managed to elude them. She then showed Juanita a graze on her arm that was caused by a bullet fired by one of them. She had kept running until she saw the house and thought she could get help there only to run into the other two men who had left the group. It was then that you came along and saved me. Juanita told her that they would remain in the woods until she came back for her as she had some business to deal with. With that Juanita headed off up the road. She did not have to go far. The other two men had obviously heard the gunfire and were heading down the road in a rickety old pickup truck. The two children were visible in the back. They were sitting back-to-back and tied together. Juanita placed herself just at the edge of the road and as soon as the vehicle was close enough, she opened fire hitting first the driver then the other in the cab. The pickup swerved off the road and came to rest on the embankment. Juanita quickly went to the back and cut the children loose and told them to follow her. Juanita took them back to where she had left Anita.

Jose arrived shortly after, and he explained that there was a lot of movement on the road, and he had heard gunfire in the distance, so he had hanged back. Juanita told him what had happened and that she wanted him to drop the children at what seemed a safe place. The children were instructed to stay down in the vehicle so they would not be visible to anyone passing by. She cautioned them strongly not to talk to anyone about what had happened.

When they arrived at what looked like a safe area Jose gave them two hundred Pesos and let them out of the vehicle.

Juanita was now dressed in a pair of jeans and a tee shirt and was looking unaffected by the excitement she had just gone through.

Jose had brought a light jacket, a small bag with personal items and a bottle of water. On seeing the water, she smiled. Her next stop was at the airport from where she would depart for Nuevo Leon and the Krystal hotel.

Early the following morning back in her hotel Juanita heard on the news about the killing of Ramon. She listened with much skepticism but not surprise as he was being portrayed as this benevolent philanthropist. Here was this sadistic drug king pin and murderer being uplifted like a saint to the people of Mexico. She thought, with this kind of attitude and fear of exposing the true nature of such a person, is there any doubt that the corruption and continuity of the drug cartels will be a protracted part of the life of the country. Instead of discouraging her from continuing her fight however it only served to give her new energy to continue her quest.

After two days in Nuevo Leon, she was ready to make her move. Juanita had not ruled out the possibility that Ciudad Juarez could become an area of interest soon due to the killing of Ramon in Tijuana. Her trip, therefore, was to be a fact-finding trip to Ciudad Juarez. She would gather information that would come in useful in case she had to make alternative arrangements in dealing with any of her proposed targets who might relocate there. While still musing on the news she got a call from Tom. "Hi, my friend, have you heard the news about what happened in Tijuana"?

"Yes, I have, and it should really put the cat amongst the pigeons don't you think"?

Tom chuckled. "Yes, it should." "And there was quite a bit of collateral damage too it seemed."

Juanita now chuckled.

"Be good my friend I am still here working on my Jamaican dialect." "See you on your return."

Just as Juanita ended the call with Tom, she heard on the news that there was now a major riot in the Aguaruto prison in Culiacan. Members of Ramon's Tijuana cartel were in pitch battle with members of the Brotherhood cartel. The Tijuana cartel members were accusing the Brotherhood of their boss Noa Gonzales arranging the murder of Ramon so that he could take over the Tijuana cartel. In the riot three prisoners were already dead and scores injured. Two prison Guards had also been killed and five injured.

Juanita smiled a pleasing smile and rubbed her hands together in satisfaction.

CHAPTER 5

Juanita arrived at the Abraham Gonzalez International Airport in the early afternoon. She immediately boarded a taxi and headed to the Hotel Santa Fe. She had originally made reservation for another hotel but minutes prior to departing Nuevo Leon she changed her booking. After a few minutes in the Taxi she directed the driver not to head directly to the hotel but instead to drive by the stadium as she wanted to have a look at it as she wanted to go to one of the games there the following day. As the taxi proceeded, she took the time to look around to spot anyone who might be following them.

Ciudad Juárez just across the Rio Grande from El Paso, Texas means different things to different people. For Juanita it would be another steppingstone on her journey towards her El Dorado or her destiny. While staying focused she would, however, take time to do a detailed study of the city and its pulsating crush of humanity. She would endeavor to blend in like a normal tourist and do what tourists do. A visit to the Plaza de Armas with the twin towers of the Cathedral of the city overlooking it like two unflinching sentries would be early on her list of places to visit. Next, she would visit the marketplace. While there were museums and galleries, they tended to have a claustrophobic effect on her so she would avoid them.

The city was established in 1659 but really began to boom during the United States prohibition. Revelers would cross the border to enjoy the city's nightlife.

Unfortunately, in the 1990 it became notorious for drug warfare as the different drug gangs fought for control of the trade in the city. As large cartels emerged, however, the ongoing feuds subsided, and the city now enjoys an uneven calm.

In touring the city Juanita chose taxis as her preferred mode of travel. This gave her independence and flexibility to chart her own course.

On the second day in the city Juanita headed to the Central Park where there is a large manmade lake. She was a bit tempted to rent one of the paddle boats and go out on the lake, but she quickly pushed that thought out of her mind. She did not want to find herself in such a vulnerable position sitting on a flimsy boat out on a lake. Instead, she satisfied herself by sitting a little distance from the edge of the lake and watch the ducks and other birds that the children were feeding as parents kept watchful eyes on them.

Her next stop that day was at the downtown market where she shopped for Mexican handicraft, clothing, and souvenirs. Shopping at the market had the advantage that it offered items made in all different parts of the country so there would be no need for her to go searching all around.

She learnt quick from her taxi driver that the art of shopping in the market was to bargain with the vendors and while she is by nature a straightforward person, she found herself enjoying the seeming game of haggling.

After a full day, Juanita returned to the Hotel Santa Fe, where she was booked. The hotel was located in the city center and near the boardwalk so once she deposited the items she had bought during the day she decided to take a walk along the boardwalk. The walk was more to facilitate her reflections on the time spent at the park. She could not get the image of the happy families siting by the shore of the lake, it brought back such sharp memories of her own family and their life in the Dominican Republic. She thought of her loving father, gentle mother and her crazy brothers getting up to all kinds of pranks. Without wanting to accept it at first but not able to deny it Juanita realized that there were tears in her eyes, which had not happened in quite a while. The tears sadness soon gave way to a sharp burning anger. Her pace quickened and she strode purposefully back to the hotel.

She showered and returned to the dining room, stopping just long enough by the bar to order a tequila sunrise which she would take to her table. On leaving the bar one overconfident gentleman detached himself from the group he was with and proceeded to approach her. He greeted her with the standard salutation which she coldly returned. Obviously not reading the body language or too confident in himself he proffered to invite her over to his table. Juanita by this time had lost her patience and any sense of humor she might had have. She said to him. "Actually, I have changed my mind I think I will dine in my room tonight it will be safer for all concerned." With that she turned and headed for her room. Juanita ordered room service and dined alone. She was savvy enough to know that once she opened herself to his invitation the next thing that would follow would be a barrage of questions about why she was in Juarez, what she did for a living, and all the things she did not want to talk about and certainly not in her present mood and state of mind. The questions would no doubt be followed by the desire to get to know her better and in her mind the usual bulls. Her plan was to spend two more days in the city gathering all the information she could, and she wanted the questioning to be coming from her. She figured she was skilled enough to extract all the information needed by seeming innocent questions to taxi drivers and others she would encounter. The bottom line is she did not want to ruin the few days left by having to think about disposing of a dead body which is what he would be if he stepped out of line.

Juanita's next two days were quite uneventful as she toured the city talking to random persons. She spoke to shoeshines, café workers, taxi drivers and even a very friendly police officer who claimed his parents were from the Trinidad and Tobago, but he had visited Dominican Republic as a boy. She took his details and promised he would hear from her. That was somewhat of a strategic move as she figured that was the best way to thwart any ideas he might be fomenting about hanging out with her. One thing she did learn from him was that the cartels were adjusting their drug trafficking activities. When pressed discretely about what was causing the shift, he opened a bit, more out of concern for his still Beloved Island of Trinidad and Tobago than out of willingness to cooperate with her. He explained that because of the tremendous pressure that the drug operations were coming under in the border regions of the United States and Mexico they are looking at diverting some of the business to European countries by way of Africa. The African route would be Mexico to Venezuela then to West African countries and through Morocco across the Gibraltar Strait and into Spain. From Spain it would fan out into other countries even as far as Russia. His concern was that in all this several Caribbean islands were now being used as transshipment areas mainly because of their close relationship with their former colonizers. He mentioned islands such as Jamaica, Antigua, Cayman and his own Trinidad and Tobago, that he confessed was what bothered him the most. It was obvious that Juanita with her innocent, but eager questions were having an impact. It was as if he was eager to inform or teach this naive female tourist what was really happening around her. Juanita was particularly curious when he mentioned that he had just heard the scuttlebutt that they were going to make a large shipment of cocaine in the next three weeks. It would be going from Venezuela to a place called Port Antonio in Jamaica and then on to the Cayman Island. He was not sure where it would go from there, but he guessed it was heading for England on a larger vessel.

CHAPTER 6

Juanita departed Ciudad Juarez for Jamaica by way of the Miami International Airport. Arriving at the Montego Bay airport at about 11:45 the same morning she was met by Kareem who whisked her away through the chaotic traffic leading out of the city.

Kareem had that impish look on his face when he turned to her and spoke. "Would you like to stop on the way to have something to eat as you are going to need all the energy when we get home."

"Really now my soldier boy you know I can give as much as I can take so be careful."

"Ok miss big talker we will see about that." "Let's stop at Scotchies and get you some of your favorite, conch soup and jerk chicken with lots of pepper."

"Ok, sounds good."

"So, did you have a productive trip"?

"Yes, it went quite well I am much more educated now on certain issues and on cultures." "And of course, I had lots of fun."

"Sounds interesting am I going to hear all about it"?

"Yes dear, you will hear it all."

The meal at Scotchies lived up to its reputation and after the meal they lingered for a while having small talk and laughing uncontrollably at the silliest of jokes.

The remainder of the trip back home was uneventful.

"Are you alright honey"? "You seem a bit distracted or deep in thought."

"Maybe just I bit jet lagged, it will pass."

"Ok, just relax and enjoy the ride, we will soon be home."

To change the topic and create a more positive atmosphere Juanita intoned. "Kareem, do you know the that one of the things that fascinate me the most when I travel and return to Jamaica is the harmonious blend of the various racial groups in the island and how everybody gets along as equal."

"Really, what brought that on now"?

"I was just thinking of the hunt we were on recently."

"What about it"?

"There we were such a diverse group getting along like old friends, when in fact we hardly knew each other." "You are Afro Jamaican, I am Hispanic and female, Gairy is Chinese, and Tom is Caucasian, but it just didn't seem to matter we felt so close and were just having an exciting time."

"That's Jamaica for you and I tell you more it's funny you brought that up because being a Jamaican I would not even have thought about it."

"I guess that's just the way things are, and we hope they remain that way forever."

Juanita spent the next few days down by her boat doing some minor repairs and chatting with her two workers. They explained that the tourist season was about to begin and so they wanted to make sure the boat was quite ready. They also suggested to her that she needed to consider doing a new set of brochures about the business. Once the brochures are done, they said they would distribute them to all the hotels and guest houses from Ocho Rios to Port Maria.

Juanita replied. "I see you gentlemen are really looking forward to a good season." "Well, I will contact the printery and have them on standby." "But first I will have to get the photographer who did the last set of pictures to come and take care of that side of things, especially since we now have the new boat."

Juanita was pleased with the people she had working with her and somehow, she got the impression that they admired her because she was businesslike and seemed like a very strong person. They were themselves very hardy young men who grew up with all the hardship that a rural community offered in Jamaica. They had grown up by the sea and had started to go to sea at an early age, so they were quite accustomed to the type of life. In addition to being fishermen some of them had gone on to learn the skills of repairing the marine engines and boat maintenance. These men were tough, hardworking, and dependable.

It is for those reasons that Juanita felt confident she could leave them in charge when she had to travel.

Having taken care of the requests of her workers in preparing for the upcoming tourist season Juanita knew that she had to make an early move again to deal with the Cayman Island drug run. She had become intrigued by it and was not going to let it go.

The day started off with its usual brilliant sunshine and gentle sea breeze wafting through the branches as it made its way up from the waters below and onto the cliff above. It was the type of Saturday morning that begged for an adventure and Juanita was up to the invitation, especially since it fitted right into her other plans. Kareem had gone to Kingston on duty and so she decided to drive to Port Antonio on a two-fold adventure. The first would be to go diving at the Lady G'Diver dive center which was located at the marina in Port Antonio. The second was to try and locate the boat would be heading to Cayman in a matter of days with a load of cocaine.

On arrival the dive center she found the operators most friendly and the business well organized. After outlining her desire, they set off in the dive boat, aptly named the Lady G. It was not long before they arrived at the dive spot and the next two hours were spent in utter bliss enjoying the underwater world with its numerous sea creatures and brilliant colors. On returning from the dive Juanita was presented with an ice-cold Red Stripe beer, which she sipped as slowly and leisurely as a flute of the most expensive champagne.

On her way from the dive shop a young boy about twelve years of age approached her and asked if she wanted to buy one of his hand-crafted wooden birds. Juanita commented that they were very pretty, she asked him the price and said she would take one. On hearing her accent, he asked. "Are you from the boat with the Spanish people"? "They bad men, I went to sell them birds, but they chased me away from the boat." "No, I am not from the boat". "Where is the boat now"? "It is on the other side of the marina miss but don't go there, they are bad men." "Thanks, my new friend, I will not go there." "By the way do you happen to remember the name of the boat"? "Yes miss, the name is Sea Sprite." "Thanks." As soon as he was out of sight Juanita did exactly what she told him she would not do. She went on a casual, carefree walk over to the nearby ice cream shop. From there she would get a better view of the area and sure enough the boat with the name Sea Sprite emblazoned on its stern was sitting there bobbing in the water. She observed for a while then decided it was time to return to her vehicle and out of the marina.

Her next stop was at Little Portie, where she had visited before and where she had met Rosie, the owner and operator. Rosie was overjoyed at seeing her and began to get all organized to pamper her and serve up some of her delicious, steamed fish.

While the meal was being prepared Juanita went on one of the rafts which operate on the river just outside the shop. By the time the raft returned her lunch was ready, so she ate and conversed with Rosie and her daughter who helps her in the shop although she was by profession a schoolteacher. Following the delicious lunch, it was time to relax on the beach nearby and just allow the time to go by.

At about 4:00 in the afternoon Juanita decided it was time to head home so she said her goodbyes and headed out.

The drive back to her cottage in Boscobel was quite uneventful except for one overambitious young driver who decided to make a fool of himself and almost lost his life doing so. Juanita on passing the vehicle parked by the side of the road under a large tree inadvertently made eye contact with the driver. That had triggered curiosity in him as she soon noticed that he had pulled out and had begun following her. She kept a steady speed and although aware of him and staying alert she gave no sign that she was bothered by his presence. When he started blowing his horn and becoming a bit of a nuisance she waited for a sufficiently long and clear stretch of road then speeded up. He took the bait and accelerated also. She slowed suddenly forcing him to brake hard. She then resumed her moderate speed while he was seen making obscene gestures to her. She thought to herself lets now have some fun if that is what you want. She speeds up just enough to tempt him in doing the same to pass her. He did not see what was coming next. As he pulled up beside her, she moved over as close as possible to his vehicle and gave him a full view of the Glock 17 she was pointing at him. In obvious panic he swerved and was last seen crashing through a banana plantation at the side of the road. That afternoon he would be contemplating extremely hard how he had underestimated his potential prey.

For the rest of the journey Juanita not wanting to take any unnecessary chances decided to stay off the main road as much as possible and used several secondary roads. The secondary roads were not ideal for driving at speed due to the numerous potholes, but she figured if he had managed to extricate himself from the banana plantation and decided to come after her he would be looking for her on the main.

When she arrived at the cottage, she was totally drained from the days' activities and the twists and turns of the side roads but on seeing Kareem the light came in her eyes and she was her sparkling deadly self again.

Juanita spent the next week seeming engrossed and totally consumed by her boating business, but her mind was far away. She was already planning a trip to the Cayman Islands. She was figured it would be a short and interesting undertaking.

CHAPTER 7

Juanita arrived in Cayman, from Jamaica, aboard Cayman Airways and headed directly to the hotel. She had made reservation at the extremely popular and beautiful Kimpton hotel in the district of West Bay. On arriving at the hotel, she immediately went to her room after which she did a quick tour of the property to orientate herself and get the lay of the compound. Having satisfied herself she went by the pool bar and ordered what has become her favorite short alcoholic drink, tequila sunrise. As she sat by the poolside working on her itinerary for the next three days, she tried to detach herself from all that was happening around while remaining alert. She could not, however, help thinking about her two recent trips to Mexico. She thought about how much some things had changed while others remained almost the same. The drug trafficking business was in a state of reinventing and reorganizing itself but was still alive and well. The country, however, was dealing with another very invasive and massive problem. The security of the country's borders were being overwhelmed by refugees fleeing their own countries and using Mexico as a true pass to enter the United States as their final destination. Some of these migrants were from other Central American countries such as Honduras, Nicaragua, and Guatemala, but more recently had been joined by persons from Haiti and as far away as West Africa. It was an arduous and journey which in some cases stretched over fifteen hundred miles from the Southern border of Mexico to the Northern border by the Rio Grande. She thought, what would happen to these people, how will Mexico manage that situation and how long could it continue like that. But mostly she wondered will many of these migrants end up as willing or unwilling participants in the drug business. She hoped not.

Juanita had noticed from her room, there was a beautiful view overlooking the ocean with its turquois water. It was no wonder then, that after a short while at the poolside she headed for her room to prepare for a leisurely swim and recline on the beach while the balmy sea breeze caressed her. This she thought was indeed paradise. After her sojourn on the beach and enduring the scrutiny of all the men she encountered Juanita retreated to her room to prepare for supper and entertainment. When she came down from her room and entered the lobby you could have heard a pin drop, there was deathly silence and it was no wonder, she would have made the goddess Aphrodite blush in amazement at her beauty. Juanita knew immediately that she would be like a lightning rod that night attracting the attention of all the hunters on the prowl. So, not wanting to be an agent provocateur she went back to her room after dinner and changed into something less provocative to the hunter's egos.

For entertainment that night she chose the Sol Y Luna club and what a night it turned out to be. She danced nonstop, going from one genre of music to the next but never more than two dances with any one partner. Then early in the morning she slipped out unnoticed and headed back to the hotel.

The following day being Saturday Juanita decided she would spend it over on the Cayman Brac which is only 20minutes away by Jet and or 45minutes on the express. She booked in at the Brac Reef Beach Resort and was most happy she did. The food was great, and the staff were super friendly, treating her like family and she enjoyed every minute of it.

The day was packed, with a host of different activities. Juanita was enjoying the relaxed, friendly atmosphere and wanted to make the most of it before returning to her life of intrigue and untold dangers. She visited the dive site of the sunken destroyer, named in honor of the late Captain Keith Tibbetts. It was a uniquely beautiful dive site. From there it was on to Rebecca's Cave. She did not do the other caves but instead went on the nature trail and finally ended up spending the rest of the evening at the beach enjoying the warm sun kissed waters. Although another visitor she had met during the tour that day tried to persuade her to have dinner at La Esperanza hotel she could not abandon her new friends at the Reef Resort, so she compromised and decided to go to La Esperanza for the entertainment after dinner.

Early the following morning Juanita was back in Grand Cayman, and she had a full day planned. She realized this was the last day she had to locate the Sea Sprite, which was her main reason for being in Cayman. After seeing the boat in Port Antonio, she had put an alert on her International Maritime Vessel Tracking site to notify her when the boat had left for Cayman. Her only loophole was that due to the small size of the Cayman Islands she was not exactly sure where it would be at anchor. It was, therefore, up to her to try and find the boat while still enjoying as much of the island as she could.

After breakfast, the first stop would be the turtle farm then it was on to stingray city and the botanical park. By mid-day it was time to slow the pace, so she decided to refresh herself by partaking of the local cuisine. She partook of turtle meat, conch and whelks all served with rice and beans and a local special known as rundown.

Her final adventure for the day would be a trip to Rum Point where she watched locals as well as visitors galivant in the water and on their boats while consuming copious amount of alcohol. Lady luck was with Juanita, as she was scanning all the boats that were anchored in the area, she saw just what she had been looking for. There was the Sea Sprite the boat that had taken her to Cayman and which she had targeted for her next anti cartel move. If all were going according to plan the boat would be carrying a substantial amount of cocaine the loss of which would be a major blow to the cartel that owns it. In addition to the significant monetary loss, however, would be the consternation about its destruction and the overall question of the network and new route that would have to be explored. That could set them back for a prolonged period as they figure out all the ramifications of the event.

Up to this point, all her other activities on Grand Cayman and Cayman Brac were just side shows to cover her moves while she searched for the Sea Sprite. The boat was anchored a little out of the close cluster of the other boats so she moved a little closer where she could observe it better and all the activities taking place onboard. She noticed there were only two men onboard and while they were drinking and enjoying the music and the general excitement, they did not allow anyone else onto their boat. After satisfying herself that she had seen enough Juanita made her way back to the hotel, changed into swimsuit and with tequila sunrise in hand headed for the pool and then a walk along the beach to relax and just take in all that had happened over the weekend. It would be a long night for her as she had business to address. While walking along the beach Juanita shook her head in disbelief and doubted her eyes for a moment. She could not believe that she was looking at the Sea Sprite now moved from Rum Point and anchored under her window just off the shore at the Public Beach. Luck was indeed being good to her, she just hoped she was not going to be as good to the men on that boat.

After having an early night Juanita got out of bed at a time when even the ghost of the infamous pirate Blackbeard would have gone to sleep. All was quiet in the hotel and the surrounding communities. She dressed in a black wetsuit and headed for the kitchen. From the kitchen she acquired a large chef's knife. She was out to do business, and this was the only weapon she could easily access. Quietly slipping out the hotel from the back, made her way down to the beach, got into the water and swam out to the boat. Climbing stealthily on board she saw one man lying prone on a bench like seat. She cautiously watched him and made her way down into the hold of the vessel. The other man she had seen earlier was nowhere in sight but what she saw and thought it might come in handy was a powerful looking speargun.

And then she spotted it, several duffle bags partially covered by a tarpaulin. She used the knife and punctured one of the bags, there she got all the proof she needed, raw cocaine.

Juanita decided that the quickest and quietest way to manage the job was to let the sea do the job. She found the thru hull fitting and manipulated it to let water into the boat so it would quietly settle to the sea floor. Just as she was going up on deck, she saw the other man entering the cabin from the jetty, she fired the spear gun directly into his chest and as he fell forward clutching the other man on the bench stirred. She turned and delivered a withering kick to his head which sent him back down on the bench and before he could collect himself, she was on him with the knife. It found its mark in his throat and one quick slashing motion ended his life in a hurry. It was now time for the hero with the spear stuck in him to be finished off. She dragged him by his collar to the top of the step leading down into the hold and slashed his throat. She made one final check to confirm that the boat was indeed flooding before slipping off into the water. Juanita then retraced her route back to the hotel where she returned the knife then headed to her room. In her room she removed the rubber gloves she wore along with her wet suit and hung them in the bathroom to be dried.

A week after returning to Jamaica, while watching the evening news on the local tv station, Juanita heard that two men were killed in a drive by shooting in Port Antonio, the men were reported to be employees at a local boat yard and the speculation was that they participated in the illegal drug trade. Later in the same news it said that a Customs officer was murdered in Grand Cayman by unknown assailants, the motive for his murder was under investigation. On hearing of these two incidents Juanita's only thought was how quickly they had retaliated for the loss of the drug and boat in Cayman. She surmised that the Customs officer had been paid for his services not to report the drugs in the boat, but the cartel might have suspected that he had leaked the information, so he had to be terminated. The same assumption pertained for the two men in Jamaica as they were the only ones who had knowledge of the drugs on the boat. Whatever their thinking, Juanita was most elated at how things were going as it would certainly cause a disruption to their operation and would force them to produce alternative plans. Having to change plans and organize new distribution network and routes is never an easy thing for the cartels. It meant they now had to recruit new personnel, find added resources, plan new methods of moving the drug from one point to the other both inland and to the destinations overseas.

Well, Juanita thought, that would be their problem I will be here to cause as much disruption as I can.

CHAPTER 8

Back in Jamaica Juanita had just wanted to slow the pace down a bit and to focus on her business and the upcoming tourist season, but where there is excitement, it always seems to find her and that was about to happen the very next day.

On arriving at the small office, she had set up in a self-contained office trailer at the port, Juanita was just about to settle down to work when one of her workers requested to see her in private.

"Come in Karl." "What's on your mind"?

"Boss some strange things are happening next door on the fishing beach."

"Ok, first thing stop with this boss stuff and tell me what is happening."

"Well Miss, for the past few days we have been noticing some strange activities taking place over there." "Last night and the night before a boat with registration from Rocky Point came here and offloaded a number of forty-five-gallon plastic barrels." "The barrels were loaded in a panel van owned by a man, by the alias name Mousie, from the Mango Valley area." "Mousie is a known drug dealer who spent time in prison in Haiti but was released last year."

"Did anyone recognize any of the people on the boat?"

"No but some of the guys who work on the boats at the beach seem to know them and are collaborating with them." "Also, two of the men on the boat seem to be Haitians."

"Miss, from what I am hearing the drugs is being kept by Mousie and one of his friends by the name of Alvin, until a boat arrives from Haiti in a day or two, at that time they will collect the drugs in exchange for guns." "Mousie seem to be the boss in charge of the operation."

"Yes, that sounds reasonable, but why don't they do that at Rocky Point?"

"The word is that Rocky Point is getting too hot as the police and the Coast Guard are now monitoring it closely."

"Ok I understand." "So do the local police for the area know about what is going on?"

"Yes, but they are a dead loss and might even be involved."

"Ok Karl, I want you to keep this information very close to your chest and do not mention it to anyone." "In the meanwhile, see if you can discretely get any more information."

Juanita took in all that Karl told her very calmly and without any indication of what she had in her mind. That evening, however, she called Andy and asked him to visit her at her home. Andy was her first employee when she started the business, and he was also privy to the mysterious explosion of a boat at the same fishing beach in the early days. She trusted Andy. The meeting with Andy was short and to the point.

"Andy, you have been with me from the beginning, and I trust you." "I have a very simple task for you, here take this phone." With that she handed him a mobile phone. "Andy, I am expecting a foreign boat to come to the fishing beach sometime between tonight and the next few nights." "I want you to keep a look out for it and the moment you see it please give me a call." "The boat is likely to be a very fast boat and will not be there at the beach for long, so we have to move real fast on it."

As far as Juanita is concerned anything to do with drugs and guns is like waving a red flag to a bull and so she was intently tempted to deal with this developing situation. In the end she relented and decided on another course of action. She was acutely aware that if she oversaw that situation, it might jeopardize not only her but her workers and the entire business.

As soon as Kareem arrived home that evening, she gave him a full report on what she had learnt and what she had put in place, and she wanted him to pass it on to his Military Intelligence people.

Kareem immediately made a phone call and planned a meeting in Ocho Rios with an operative from the Intelligence unit. In two hours, he and Juanita headed for Ocho Rios. On arriving there he dropped Juanita at the Shaw Park Hotel and went on to the meeting further in the town.

The meeting ended as quickly and unceremoniously as it began. They both agreed that there was much to be done in a truly brief time. They also agreed that Juanita would have no more involvement in the operation, for her own safety. On the way back home, Kareem explained what had happened and that she was not to get involved anymore except for possible information about the arrival of the boat and that she was to pass that to him only. Juanita was literally pinching herself for telling Kareem about the operation and not doing it herself. On reaching home she calmed herself down with a Tequila Sunrise followed by a glass of red wine. When Kareem asked her if she was all right, she rolled her eyes and spoke. "Are you not lucky that you have such a good girl to put you to bed and put up with your always going away to play soldier and leaving me alone in that lovely house with only the sound of the wind at night." She smiled a mischievous smile then he answered.

"Who is talking about leaving anyone alone, oh my goodness the gypsy has a nerve I was just thinking I might have to put one of those anchors you have on your boat around your waist to keep you grounded so I can catch up with you."

"Ok let's go make music now we will call it the soldier and the gypsy." With that she took him by the buckle of his belt and walking backways pulled him into the bedroom.

Two nights after the meeting with Kareem and the operative Juanita got a call from an extremely excited Andy.

"The boat is here; it's just making its way through the channel and up to the jetty right now." "It looks like a very fast boat mam; it has three giant outboard engines."

"Ok Andy thanks and you can relax now."

Within a few minutes of docking the panel van made its way onto the jetty and immediately all hell seemed to break loose. Two military helicopters flying nap of the earth suddenly appeared at the beach and started landing soldiers who were joined by other soldiers who suddenly appeared from an ambulance that had arrived nearby a few minutes before. To complete the picture the Coast Guard cutter appeared from around the bluff where it had been lying in wait.

Unknown even to Juanita was the fact that the boat was being tracked by satellite from the time it entered Jamaican waters. That information was being constantly updated to the Air wing and the soldiers involved.

The following day Juanita again cautioned both Karl and Andy to act normal and not to discuss the night's happenings with anyone but at the same time they should keep their ears open and stay alert.

In the end Juanita was glad she did not take on the task and was happy for the outcome. Any blow to drug traffickers was a victory for her.

Kareem was intently focused on the road ahead through the fading light of the evening, as he made his way home from the rugby match in Kingston and to his lovely Juanita. Suddenly out of nowhere a small truck appeared in his rearview mirror seemingly travelling at an exceedingly high rate of speed. To prevent a mishap, he pulled as far off the road as he could to let the truck go by, but that was not to be, the truck slammed into his car and sent him careening over the low embankment and into the small river below. He fought with all his might to control the vehicle, but it was to no avail. Finally, it came to rest against a large boulder in a sandy section of the river just out of the water. He quickly extricated himself from his seatbelt and the airbag which had been deployed and got away from the vehicle fearing that there might be an explosion. Much to his ease of mind there was no explosion, so he returned to it and got out his firearm and other important items he had inside. By this time, a small group of people had gathered and were in amazement that he was still alive and not severely injured. Although a bit shaken by the incident he inquired of the crowd if they had seen the truck that had hit him as it was nowhere in sight.

One of the drivers who had stopped up on the road above offered him a ride to the nearest police station so he could make a report. On the way to the station, he called Juanita to inform her of what had happened and at the same time reassured her that he was all right and that the police had offered to take him home.

The police on receiving his report surmised that either the act was intentional, the driver of the truck engaged in something illegal, or the truck might have been stolen. The matter would, however, be thoroughly investigated. Kareem, then arranged with the police to have a tow truck go and recover the vehicle before it was scrapped by unscrupulous individuals.

Early the next day, although not having any major problems, Kareem decided that, out of an abundance of caution, he would see the doctor to confirm that all was well. He had x-rays done and a few other checks but was dismissed with the advice to take three days off from work and not to undertake any strenuous activities.

On leaving the doctor he went to the garage where the vehicle had been taken and contacted his insurance company.

While Kareem was satisfied to treat the accident as just that, Juanita would not and so she decided to discretely follow any trail that would lead her to the person responsible.

Alvin Nesbet was always a loudmouth, and it was that mouth that was about to seal his faith.

Three days after the accident someone reported to Corporal Bennett at the police station that they had the license number of the truck that was involved in the accident but was hesitant to come forward because she had heard rumors that the owner was involved with the person who was recently arrested for the drug bust at the marina in Oracabessa recently. She only decided to report it because her husband had encouraged her to do so and had instructed her to speak only to Corporal Bennett as he was his friend from school days, and he could be trusted.

Before Corporal Bennett could act on the information, Alvin was seen in a bar in Mango Valley drinking and mouthing off what he had done and that it was all to avenge the boss who had been arrested. He wanted to send a message that no outsider can come into the area and work against them with police and soldiers. He had convinced himself that Kareem being a soldier had arranged the raid on them and how lucky he was that he did not die in the accident.

"But there will be another time and this time he won't be so lucky."

Word travels extremely fast in small rural communities and so it was no surprise that people were openly talking about it down by the marina and even in the hearing of Juanita.

Alvin was hence forth marked for death, but the date for him to meet his demise would have to be put on hold for some time as moving too quickly could have negative repercussions. The last thing Juanita wanted at this time was for it to seem like a revenge killing, as is so prevalent on the island.

For now, Alvin would continue to enjoy life on top of the grass.

CHAPTER 9

After three months in Jamaica, Juanita prepares to leave for Mexico to deal with the Brotherhood cartel in Culiacan

On her return to Nuevo Leon, Mexico Juanita did not return to the Crystal hotel but instead booked into the more upscale Safi Royal Luxury hotel across from the Plaza Fiesta. The area nestled between mountains to the North and South and gave the impression of being in the palms of two large hands. Juanita must surely be thinking of returning to this beautiful place sometime in the future with Kareem, just to relax and enjoy the pleasantries of life. But for now, it was time to get on with this business.

Her next move would be to take down Noa Gonzales the head of the brotherhood cartel, which is based in Culiacan, Sinaloa.

If all goes as Juanita envisages when she takes out Noa it will touch off a wave of panic and infighting, as successors in both the Tijuana and now the brotherhood cartels fight for control, that will result in such a chaotic situation that the government would be forced to deploy all its resources to put an end to the situation and preserve the country from descending into complete anarchy.

Juanita arrived at the Culiacan International Airport late in the evening and headed directly to the Hotel Lucerna across the Rio Tamazula which runs through the city from East to West. This location placed her thirteen miles from the ranch where Noa Gonzales had established his headquarters.

The ranch was to the south of the small town of Laguna Colorada and just east of the Culiacan aerodrome, which he used frequently for his business trips, and highway 15.

Culiacán, is the capital of and the largest city in Sinaloa. It was founded on September 29, 1531, by the Spanish explorers.

It is located 1,240 km from Mexico City, and 1,159 km from Tijuana to the North.

The city is well known for its culture, luxuries, and celebrations. Its numerous sites of interest include its historic center, Las Riberas Park, the dancing fountains and religious temples such as its Basilica Cathedral, the sanctuary, and the Lomita. The modern Tres_Ríos district is known for its buildings, squares, hotels, parks, restaurants, schools, etc.

The population is made up of nationals from many different countries including Americans, Canadians, Italians, Greeks, Cubans, Chinese, Japanese, Russians, Ukrainians, Germans, among others.

There is a large Greek population which is believed to be the largest Greek community in Mexico.

The city itself seems to be divided into different zones. There is the Historical Center of Culiacan which is the original area of the city, in which most of the buildings of the Spanish colonization between the 16th and 19th centuries are found. During the '70s there was a depopulation of the area due to the prohibitive costs of rents, traffic congestion and the need for more commercial spaces. In recent years, however, there has been a process of repopulation boosted by the construction of apartments in the periphery of the Center and a project of urban reorganization in which it is intended to have a higher population density.

The other area outside the Historical Center is Las Colonias, which are the first settlements that created somewhat of a perimeter around the original urban area. This allowed people from different social strata to have a wide space to settle close to the Center.

The third areas are the Residentials that are areas strategically built for people with high purchasing power. These areas have spacious houses, large green areas and in most cases, they are delineated as private. It is in one such area that Noa Gonzales established his ranch.

Culiacán's economy is agricultural and commerce, being a trade center for produce, meat, and fish. Among other industries, Culiacán represents thirty two percent of the state economy.

There is however another dark side to the economy of the region. Beginning in the late 1950s, Culiacán became the birthplace of an insidious and pervasive underground economy based on illicit drugs exported to the United States. The completion of the Pan-American Highway and the regional airport in the 1960s greatly contributed to the development of the trade by expanding the distribution network. The Sinaloa Cartel, a drug trafficking and organized crime syndicate made Culiacán its primary base. The brotherhood cartel under Noa Gonzales is a continuation of that cartel.

On this trip Juanita would not indulge much in visiting places of interest but would be lazar focused on the task ahead and how best to accomplish her objective.

From all the information gathered Noa was well protected by the local folks and the ranch was well fortified. There were numerous security cameras around the main house and the stables and there were security guards on duty around the clock.

Juanita realized that this would possibly be her most challenging mission to date but there was no turning back. The key was to find the weakness in his armor and exploit it.

On the second day in Culiacan Juanita discovered that every Thursday at 8:00 A.M. sharp Noa flew out of Culiacan aerodrome to Mazatlán international airport in the south, to attend a horse show at Villa Union. Juanita mused that her best option was to strike somewhere along that journey but where, when, and how. Realizing that Thursday was only two days away she spent the next day reconnoitering the area and weighing her options.

The idea came like a bolt, unexpectedly, but in the same way it came in the same way she concluded that she needed her trusted assistant Jose Vargas to facilitate her.

Jose Vargas was born in the town of Tapachula at the southernmost part of Mexico at the border with Guatemala. He was from a modest family where his father worked as a travelling salesman selling children's books from his van while his mother was a stay-at-home mom who kept herself busy in her vegetable and flower garden. As a boy, when he was out on holidays from school, he would accompany his dad on trips all over the nearby towns and villages. At the age of eighteen when he graduated from high school, he joined the police force and after two years he was trained as undercover police and transferred to the town of Monterrey in the state of Nuevo Leon as a member of the of the drug squad. While collaborating with the squad he was at one point embedded with a drug cartel and gained significant knowledge about their operations. Juanita considers him one of the most resourceful and diligent persons she had ever operated with. He was a quick thinker and could sense danger a mile away.

She now reached out to him to provide her with supplies she would need to complete her mission.

The morning was sunny and bright with a brisk wind blowing from the hills to the east as if to clear the area of the specter of death that was about to unleash its fury in the otherwise quiet community. At 7:40 A. M. Noa Gonzales exited his house and went to his vehicle. His driver and one man, possibly a bodyguard, were with him. Juanita was happy with that; she did not want a repeat of what had happened when she had taken out Elan Morales. On that occasion she had just taken the second pressure on the trigger when she saw his little daughter running towards him in the same moment his head had exploded from the bullet that had found its mark from her sniper's rifle twelve hundred meters away.

Satisfied that all was in order, she drove slowly past Noa's entrance to his home from the main road. She watched through her rearview mirror and timed it perfectly when he about to egress his property onto the road, she triggered the device and kept going. The quiet of the morning was shattered by a tremendous explosion which could be heard all around the neighboring communities. The explosion had lifted the vehicle into the air just before it burst into flames. Juanita just kept going.

On her arrival back at the hotel the staff and guests were huddled in little groups speculating on what might have happened. One person who appeared to be a police officer muttered that it seems as if the drug don had met his fate, but he followed up with the dire warning that somebody will pay dearly for that if caught by his followers.

Juanita spent the rest of the day by the pool pretending to be engrossed in a book about sea life. The book was a mere ploy to confuse any who might be curious about her, in the same way she did not check out of the hotel and leave the area the same morning.

The following morning after breakfast she checked out of the hotel and was on her way to Nuevo Leon and the Safi Royal Luxury hotel.

She spent one day in Nuevo Leon then departed for Miami and on to Jamaica.

The next six months in Jamaica Juanita followed the news of what was happening in the drug war in Mexico very closely. As she had predicted there was much chaos and infighting within the cartels as persons fought for the top positions. While at the same time there was fighting for dominance of regions between the various cartels.

CHAPTER 10

One bit of news she received stirred her interest and had her perplexed to the point she made a call to the police officer she had met on her trip to Ciudad Juarez. She told him that she had heard on the news that things were getting a bit tense in the region, so she was checking to see that he was safe and still doing an excellent job. Her call had just the effect she intended and soon he was rattling on about all that was taking place.

Juanita had heard that following the death of Angelo Palomino the leader of "La familia Nueva and Ramon Mendoza the leader of the Tijuana cartel Alejandro Quintin had moved to Juarez and established the Los Fuegos Cartel.

Los Fuegos Cartel formerly operated in the region just north of the capital Mexico City. While Alejandro was overall in charge, he allowed some smaller associated cartels to own separate but cooperating organizations. Because of that structure Los Fuegos Cartel had connections from New York City to Buenos Aires and every major city in between.

It would not be long before Juanita's actions would begin to take their toll on the drug trafficking business.

The termination of the top cartel leaders the infighting and government now seizing the initiative to crackdown was becoming oppressive. So, Alejandro handed over the reins of Los Fuegos cartel to Salvador Nunez and fled. Salvador would be Juanita's next target. She was determined to keep hitting them until they became frustrated to the point of having second thoughts about the business.

To conduct this mission Juanita traveled from Montego Bay, Jamaica to Atlanta, Georgia then on to Ciudad Juarez. She traveled by taxi to the hotel Lucerna where she had made reservation. Juanita planned to be in Juarez for no longer than three days and then be on her way back to Jamaica.

On arriving at the hotel, she kept an extremely low profile, choosing to have room service rather than eat dinner in the dining room. Even when room service arrived, she did not meet face to face with the staff but watched discretely from the bathroom.

This mission was to be a quick and clean one, with no personal contact with the target.

In conducting her due diligence and follow up reconnaissance Juanita had located the popular night club that was owned by her target, Salvador Nunez.

It was no surprise the following night that she arrived just minutes after Nunez had arrived at the club. Behind the scenes significant activities had taken place. Jose had placed a tracking device on Nunez's vehicle and so it was over to Juanita to track him when she was ready to make her move. Jose had also made a dead drop of a bomb in a small, wooded area a short distance to the northeast of the Olympic stadium. The bomb was fully assembled except for the detonator which was hidden by Jose in the rental vehicle being used by Juanita. Once she collected the drop, she would be able to accomplish the task.

Juanita arrived at the club in a taxi rather than her rental vehicle. It was all a part of the plan.

On arrival and exiting the taxi she looked around to ensure no one was around. She then attached the bomb to the under belly of the target vehicle, having armed it before, and walked into the club. In the club she went into the restroom and once alone changed from the wrap-around skirt and removed the light blue jacket and blond wig she was wearing. Her high heels were replaced by a fashionable

Mexican sandal. She was now dressed in a very tight-fitting pair of shorts and a Mexican souvenir tee shirt which accentuated he well-toned body. She ordered one drink at the bar and stayed there just long enough to be noticed then she exited through the front door rather than the side door through which she had entered. As soon as she exited the club she went into a taxi and collected a parcel that Jose had sent. She drove for about ten minutes to another club and went inside. In that club another transformation took place, she was now wearing a flaming red wig, a black jacket, and black jeans. But most significantly she had gotten the tip off from Jose that the target had entered his vehicle, so she remotely triggered the device that was placed under it. Nunez was now history. After a brief stay it was time to call it a night, so she took another taxi and got out one street over from where she had parked her rental vehicle. She got in and made one final change by getting rid of her red wig and returning to the appearance she had checked in at the hotel with.

Just before going to sleep, she saw on the late news that another bombing had taken place in the city.

The trip back home this time was a bit circuitous, going from Mexico to Trinidad onto Barbados and finally Jamaica.

Kareem was not at the airport to meet her, but he had arranged for a friend to do so.

John was a good friend and former school mate of Kareem, and while unlike Kareem he did not join the military they remained close over the years. He was an avid shooter and a member of the island's rifle association which he represents in pistol and full-bore shooting competitions. That was in fact one of the factors that keep him and Kareem in close contact as they often met in competitions and at association meetings.

Juanita had met him before and was always impressed by his quiet and easy-going demeanor. She often thought that if she wanted to put together a sniper team he would definitely be in it.

When they got arrived at the cabin Juanita offered John a drink while she went inside to change and freshen up. When she got out of her room. She found John standing on the deck looking out to the sea below and in the distance.

"Hi John, what are you thinking?"

"Just admiring the beauty of the sea and its restless energy."

"Would you like to go out for a ride on the boat?" "It is a beautiful day for it."

"Most certainly, I would never pass up such an offer."

"Ok then, let me call Andy and have him prepare the boat."

"He will call me when all is ready so in the meanwhile just take in the scenery."

While waiting John spoke about his last shooting competition in Guyana. In that competition he emerged the top pistol shot, and the team came in second overall. In the full-bore shoot, however, he again topped it and the team took the top spot.

Andy called about an hour later, and they headed down to the jetty.

They had just navigated the narrow channel through the offshore reef and had been cruising around for about thirty minutes. Juanita had given John the helm and was coaching him in what was unusually calm water.

Juanita saw a boat detach itself from all the other boats in the area and was coming at her boat at a rapid speed just off the starboard bow. She instantly took control from John and instinctively turned her boat into the approaching boat. It was a sturdily built wooden canoe, such as those used by the fishers who go far out to sea. It was outfitted with two exceptionally large outboard engines. As the boat flashed by her starboard side, she saw one man stand in the canoe and heard two gunshots.

Her next move was a hard turn to port so as not be caught up in his wake. She continued the wide turn. As she was in that turn the canoe made a turn to starboard and was now approaching on her port bow. She continued to turn towards the canoe and made it come towards her. The canoe was much faster but was lower in the water, these Juanita thought would be factors to be exploited.

Consistent with her maneuvering John was bracing himself against the side of their boat with his pistol by his side but just out of sight of those in the canoe. As the canoe got to a short distance of her port bow Juanita suddenly cut her engine to a stop. As she did so the canoe flashed by and John fired three shots, two into the person with the weapon and one into the rear of the boat. The shot to the stern must have hit one of the engines as it promptly exploded taking with it the other engine and the rear end of the canoe. The person who had been driving the canoe was now swimming for his life, so she sailed over, and Andy who was now up from the bottom of the boat, where he had been taking cover, pulled him aboard. The other boats in the area all began to gather around in astonishment at what had just taken place. Juanita sailed to the jetty and handed over the man to the police then she proceeded to the police station with John to give their account of what had happened. It was only at this point that she heard that the other man in the canoe who John had shot was Alvin the same man who had forced Kareem's vehicle off the road while he had been on his way back from Kington.

Alvin must have been plotting his move beforehand and was awaiting what he thought would be the right opportunity to hit back. He did but it did not end well for him.

After finishing at the police station Juanita went to the jetty where Andy was busily inspecting the boat for damage. She told him not to do any repairs until the police had inspected it.

Before leaving the jetty, she said to Andy. "Andy my man your life is always full of excitement when you are around me, isn't that so?"

"Yes, mam that is true, but I love it."

On the way back to the house John turned to her and spoke. "I had no idea a trip to the airport could be this exciting."

Juanita intoned. "Stick around and you will be surprised I am like a lightning rod."

"Thanks for letting me know."

When Kareem arrived that evening Juanita and John recounted their adventure with John embellishing it significantly. Juanita had a hearty laugh while Kareem responded. "John you always had a vivid imagination but this time I think you have outdone yourself." "Liar." They all laughed.

CHAPTER 11

Early this morning Juanita got a call from Jose, who was vacationing in Trinidad. He told her that the cartels were in a state of enormous panic because of the recent eliminations of the heads of major cartels. He said a number of the cartels had fragmented beyond recognition. Some main players in the business had opted to leave Mexico completely. The majority of those had headed to the United States and Canada where most of their money was already stashed away. Others had simply relocated to countries such as Venezuela, Guyana, Jamaica and even Haiti. The move to Haiti was particularly interesting to Juanita because of the instability of that country but she knew it was somewhere that could be easily exploited, not only, because of the rampant poverty and unemployment existing there but because of the abundance of firearms in the country.

Jose also informed her that Alejandro Quintin had quietly slips out of Mexico with his family by private jet. They head to The Gambia then Morocco and on to Spain. It was his hope to spend the rest of his days there but unfortunately the wake he had left behind had not quietly vanished in the following seas. He was already marked with an indelible curse.

As Juanita sat sipping her coffee and pondering all that Jose had told her she got a phone call. It was Kareem.

"Hi sweetheart, what have you been up to?"

"Nada en realidad."

"That sound unlike you, I can bet your brain is working overtime."

"Anyway, I have been thinking."

"Wow! You have been thinking."

"Come on don't be rude, at least you know I think about you, I have to because I hardly see you."

"Ok rub it in."

"Honey I have been thinking that we have not really travelled overseas together, and I would like to change that."

"That is true my man." "What did you have in mind?"

"Well, I have some leave coming up and it would be wonderful to take a vacation together and what better time than now with all that has been happening recently." "You must be a bit stressed and frankly I could do with a break from work and to spend some quality time with you."

"That sounds like an excellent idea." "Where did you have in mind?"

"Well, I was going to leave that up to you."

"You know I am normally a quiet girl but when it's time to have fun I can become quite an action junkie at the drop of a hat."

"You and I have been travelling a lot on this side of the world, so how about a European trip." "We could start in the England then on to France and end up in Spain." "I understand Spain is beautiful in autumn."

"Sounds like an excellent idea I will put in for my leave in the next two weeks, then we should be ready to go in a month."

An excellent idea indeed it was but for whom.

While Kareem went about his daily duties and waiting for his application to be approved Juanita continued with her boat business as normal. Ideas, however, were twirling around in her head at a high rate of speed. Juanita was there in Jamaica, but her mind was already in Spain. She had a mission on her mind. But all in its own time, after all, their vacation in Europe would not be for another month.

In order to keep up with things in Mexico and also to pass the time as Kareem would be on assignment in Montego Bay for the next week, Juanita made a call to her police contact in Ciudad Juarez.

"Hello mi amigo, how are things?" "Just calling to check on you that you are safe and staying out of trouble."

"Hello, good to hear from you and yes I am safe although that is very hard to do here."

"What's happening there now?"

"Well things are becoming extremely dangerous now since the death of the head of the Los Fuegos cartel." "The different factions of the cartel were becoming very suspicious of each other, and the trust level was exceptionally low."

"So, who is running the show now?"

"Ricardo Diaz is the new head he took over following the death of Salvador Nunez has been trying his best to maintain control."

"It seems that he as the overall head of the group is now planning something." "The word on the street was that they are still smarting from the loss of the shipment to Cayman and so they were about to try a different routing."

"Any idea where that might be headed?"

"It seems that the route will be again from Mexico to Venezuela however, no one seems to know where it will go from Venezuela."

"Word also is that Tony Diaz the number two man and brother of Ricardo Diaz will be directly involved."

"Thanks again my friend and you continue to stay safe."

"I will do my best but tell me something why are you so interested in this stuff?"

"Well, you are my friend, and I am concerned about you, plus it is a part of my job."

"I don't remember you telling me what you do." "What exactly do you do?"

"I am studying the impact of such things as violence and natural disasters on migration." "That is also the reason why I have to travel so much." "It is hard but interesting work but on the plus side I get to meet good people like you."

"Wow! That does sound interesting, I hope we will meet again soon."

"Thanks, and I hope so too, in the meanwhile you take care and be safe."

Two days after speaking to her police contact in Juarez Juanita got a call from Dominic in the Dominica Republic.

"Juanita, it seems there is a major drug run being planned between Haiti and Jamaica and I thought you would be interested in it."

After he outlined what he had heard about the possible shipment she became more than interested.

Dominic told her that the shipment would be different from the straight drug for gun trade that normally goes on between Jamaica and Haiti.

"This transaction is not the normal where marijuana flows out of Jamaica in exchange for guns out of Haiti." "This trip, involve cocaine, guns and a number of young girls being trafficked from Haiti to Jamaica and marijuana coming from Jamaica to Haiti."

"The guns would remain in Jamaica while the cocaine and the girls would be headed to other destinations."

To say that Juanita was incensed by this information would be an understatement, she was livid with anger.

Dominic did not have exact date for the shipment to take place, but he promised that he would monitor the situation and give a call when it was ready. He further mentioned that the human trafficking was mainly a collaboration between the cartel and a criminal gang in Haiti, and that along with kidnappings were their ways of funding their operations and their gun purchases.

Following the call from Dominic and the other information she had received Juanita called Jose and requested that he try to find out all he could from his end and especially what was going on with the Los Fuegos cartel.

When Jose called back two days later, he confirmed all that had been said by the police from Juarez and he also confirmed that Tony Diaz would be traveling incognito to Haiti by air and then he would move with the boat involved in the trafficking from Haiti to Jamaica. Once in Jamaica he would be taken to a safe house along with the girls to await their next move out of the island. At this point, however the girls would go a separate way than he and the cocaine.

Juanita now rationalized that the information given by Dominic tied in with that from Mexico, so it was now up to her to formulate a plan. She was determined that this time she would manage it by herself and only involve the Jamaican police when absolutely necessary. It was a rather precarious position she was about to put herself in, but she was determined.

Juanita now needed to identify the possible safe house in Jamaica and how best to deal with the safety of the girls who would be involved. She was also hoping that all would happen quickly as it had to happen before her trip to Europe with Kareem.

A week later Juanita was confident she had all the information she needed on her side to plan, she only needed to wait on the call from Dominic informing her of the movement of the boat.

The call came two days later and immediately Juanita began her preparations and set off for Kingston. From there she timed herself to arrive at the spot she planned to leave her vehicle and make her way to the safe house using the cloak of darkness and the nearby forest.

The boat would be leaving from Les Anglais in Haiti and would arrive at Foule Bay, St. Thomas Jamaica at about 2:00 A.M. The safe house was in a wooded area to the West of Amity Hall village. Juanita was waiting among the trees to the side of the building. She was patient yet anxious. This was the first operation she had gotten involved in that actually involved so many different individuals and it gave her some cause for concern. She had to be extremely careful. For the operation she was dressed in black jump suit with a hoody and total face covering.

She could not see the spot the boat would dock so she would have to estimate the time of arrival and the time it would take for the vehicle to arrive at the house. While she waited Juanita realized that there was one man left behind at the house, but she would let him live for now.

At 2:45 A.M. Juanita saw the white panel van driving up the narrow dirt road to the house. She grew extremely tense as she waited for the right moment to strike.

As soon as it arrived the driver blew his horn once and flashed the head lights twice, a light came on in the house. The driver got out of the van and moved around to the back. He tapped on the door three times then opened it. As it opened one man came out and there was the whimpering of girls inside. Juanita sprang into action, with silencer on her Glock pistol she dropped the two men at the back of the van, then moving cat like she advanced to the passenger side of the front of the vehicle and shot the two men in the passenger seats. The one nearest the door had been in the act of stepping out when he met the sudden impact of her bullet. The other was still reaching for his weapon when he too was terminated. No sooner than she had shot him she saw the door of the house open, and a man was about to emerge, he got it full in the chest and went down. Juanita then went to the back of the vehicle where she saw the girls huddled together with their arms bound. In broken Creole and Spanish, she quickly instructed them to follow her to the edge of the tree line. Once there Juanita, cut the bonds from their hands and directed them towards a church which was just a short distance away. There she told them to wait for the police who would soon take them to safety. She also charged them to say that they were rescued by two men, but they did not say who they were, they just came out of nowhere, shot the men and released us, then they disappeared just as suddenly as they came.

A quick look around the vehicle revealed a number of boxes of drugs and firearms. They were covered with plastic wrapping. Juanita was also able to identify the man in the middle seat, by the tattoo on his chest which was discernable despite being covered by blood, he was Tony Diaz the number two man in the Los Fuegos cartel. This would be another major blow to them.

Juanita slashed all the tires of the vehicle then slipped back into the woods where she made a phone call to Dominic in Dominica. The call was short and to the point.

"I am done here, make the call."

"I will my friend, be careful."

She was sorry she could not have destroyed the drugs and guns herself, but she hoped the police would get there in a hurry once she had called Dominic. He was to put the finishing touches on the operation. Juanita had given Dominic the direct phone number for the Jamaican Police Commissioner. Dominic would tell him about the drug and the guns and give direction to the safe house, he would also tell him about the girls who should be at the Amity Hall Friends church and about the boat that would be on its way back to Haiti with the marijuana. The Commissioner it was expected would then act expeditiously in dispatching officers from the Morant Bay police to go to the site and also inform the Coast Guard about the boat so they could try and intercept it.

Following her call to Dominic, Juanita stealthily made her way to the place she had left her vehicle, then using the main road she headed back home by way of Pt. Antonio rather than through Kingston as she did on her way out for the operation.

On the way back home, Juanita again started to reflect on the number of people who she interacted with for the operation, and she began to question her judgement. The journey back home was uneventful and after a quick shower and a vodka she was ready for a long sleep.

Juanita had hardly opened her eyes when the phone rang.

"Hi honey, how are you?"

"I am good, just about to make my coffee." "How is it in Montego Bay?"

"Things are going well but I miss you."

"I understand dear, things have been very quiet on this side."

"No more boat race and shootout at sea?"

"Very funny Kareem, you will pay for that when you get home."

"That's what I like to hear, I will take my punishment like a real man." "Okay will call you later."

"Have a good day honey."

"Oh! Did you hear about some shooting in St. Thomas last night?"

"No Kareem, I didn't." "What happened?"

"Seems as there was some kind of drug trafficking transaction that went bad, about five men were killed." "That is all I know so far; I will fill you in on the details when I hear more."

"Okay honey you do that." "I will be doing some work down by the office today and also cleaning up the boats."

"Okay be safe."

Juanita finally got her coffee and went to sit on the deck. While there she began to reflect on what had happened just hours ago. She then gave Dominic a call to fill him in on the details. He was extremely excited.

"Sounds like you had a good night Juanita, I will be keeping my ears close to the ground to pick up what I can from this side." "Based on what you have said it sounds like all hell will break lose soon, starting in Mexico then Haiti and Jamaica."

"Yes, I am expecting that." "Well keep me updated when you hear anything I need to go back to bed to get my beauty sleep."

"That I can assure you that you don't need but go get your rest, we will talk."

"Are you trying to flatter me young man?" "Well, it's working." "You be good and go get some rest yourself."

"Okay bye."

CHAPTER 12

Having put all her thoughts together on how she would execute her plan to eliminate Alejandro Quintin the former leader of the Los Fuegos cartel Juanita was determined to move with urgency on it. In her possession she had a picture of her target and the house he was occupying with his family in Spain. All had been going well. She had talked Kareem into visiting Spain as a part of a European vacation, and here they were now. She had tracked down and located her target. It was now time to act. Her only problem now was how to get away from Kareem for the time she would need to undertake her mission without arousing his suspicion.

The opportunity presented itself through another guest they had met at the hotel while at dinner one night. Gena was a British girl on business in Madrid where they were, and she and Juanita had hit it off quite well as all three of them chatted after dinner. At one point Gena and Juanita left for the lady's room and it was then that Gena told Juanita that she would be heading out of Madrid for a few days. This was the opportunity Juanita would seize upon. Knowing that she and Kareem were due to leave Spain in two days Juanita decided to put her plan into action.

The day before leaving Spain, Juanita told Kareem that Gena had invited her on a girl's shopping trip so she would be linking up with her downtown that afternoon.

The following day while on the train Juanita was busy admiring the scenery as it flashed by outside, then she began to focus on the passengers inside the train and it was then that she caught sight of the man sitting a few seats down from her.

The man had a little girl that must have been his daughter sitting with him, she clung to him so tightly and was obviously having much fun with him as she pointed out things through the window. They were both so happy and engaged with each other. The interaction brought back vivid memories to Juanita of the times she was with her father and the friendship they shared. The memories brought back a flood of emotion. But that scene also had another cruel and piercing impact on her. That picture of the man and his daughter took her mind to the picture of the man she was on her way to terminate, in that picture her target also had his little daughter cuddling him. The final twist of the emotional dagger came, however, when it took her memory back to when she had shot Elan Morales Garcia just as his little daughter was running towards him. She remembered how his head had exploded in front of the child. She had squeezed the trigger just a fraction of a section prior to seeing the child. Juanita sat as if transfixed for a while then she decided. For the first time she would abort a mission. She got off the train at the next stop and took the return train to the hotel.

Back at the hotel she ran inside and threw her arms around Kareem and started to sob.

"Hi honey what's the matter, are you all right?"

"Yes, sweetheart I am all right just some change of plans and I wanted to be back here with you. I love you very much."

Juanita was most skilled at hiding her true feelings and of deflecting searching questions.

"Wow! For a moment you had me worried I thought you had run into the running of the bull's festival."

"Kareem you are so funny." "Let's change and go relax by the pool."

"Okay sounds good to me." "After that you could probably get a massage to prepare you for the long trip back home."

CHAPTER 13

Back in Jamaica, Juanita confessed to Kareem that she needed to make a short trip to her home country, the Dominican Republic. She told him that she needed some time to clear her head about a few things related to her past.

"Honey are you sure you don't want me to accompany you on this trip?"

"That would be nice Kareem and I assure you that one day we will visit together, but this is something I need to do alone."

"Okay I understand."

On arriving in Dominica, she was picked up at the airport by Dominic. They spent the rest of the afternoon together and late in the evening he took her to his house to meet with his parents who knew her as a child. It was a very pleasant reunion; they showed much excitement in seeing her again.

Dominic's mom asked. "So, what have you been doing with yourself, you look very well?"

"Well following the death of my family, I got out of the military in the United States and did a lot of travelling around." "It was as if I was in search of myself." "The death of your family was quite a shock to all of us and we were very saddened by it." "Well, we are just happy to know that you are okay and looking well."

"Thanks much, it was difficult at first, but I found my way."
"Then on one of my many trips I met a young man who is in the Jamaican military, and we connected so well I ended up in Jamaica."

"So, what are you doing there in Jamaica?"

"I actually own a small boating business on the North Coast of the island in the tourist area." "I started with one boat taking tourists out to dive sites and just boating around, now I have two boats and a very good work crew, so I am planning to expand in the near future."

"That sounds very good, and with your drive I am sure you will do well."

"Well, I have to get back to the hotel now, so Dominic if you don't mind will you be a good lad and be my chauffer."

"Anytime fair Princess."

"Be careful son she is already taken; I don't know why you didn't snag her first."

Everyone laughed as they headed to the door.

The next day Dominic picked her up and took her to the burial site of her parents. She asked hm to leave her for about an hour and then return.

In the cemetery Juanita sat on the grave of her father and wept. She then assured them that she had fulfilled her promise to them about getting justice for them. She said it was now time to put her past behind her and focus on a more positive lifestyle.

Dominic came back for her, and they had lunch together. He then dropped her at the hotel where she freshened up and took a taxi to the airport.

On the trip back to Jamaica she was in a melancholy mood but nevertheless felt like a great load had been lifted off her shoulder.

Kareem was overjoyed to see her and after a prolonged hug and show of affection they got into his vehicle and headed for the cottage.

CHAPTER 14

Once she had returned from the DR Juanita got down to working on her business. The boats had been kept in immaculate condition and so she began to focus fully on advertising and visiting the hotels in the region to create and reinforce the links with them so that they would direct business her way.

While her main focus was on the development of the business, she decided to get more involved with the surrounding communities. To that end she would visit the various villages and interact with the elderly folks, especially the ladies. She also began visiting some of the primary schools and gave them books and other needed school supplies. In a truly abbreviated time, she was extremely popular in the area with the school children. It soon became quite common to see her at the schools teaching the girls some basic self-defense to protect themselves. This made her even more popular with the girls and soon the boys began to feel left out and asked her if they could be included. She yielded and they joined her group.

In all of this community outreach Juanita had a plan. She was in effect creating a protective network around her. This network would serve to inform her of any adverse feelings or threats that might surface from outsiders.

Juanita had made one of her usual visits to a school in a rural village and was on her way back home when she stopped by the roadside to take pictures of an unusual rock formation. Just as she was finished and going back towards her vehicle, she saw two young men approaching. She was not in the least apprehensive and very calmly greeted them. At this point the one dressed in jeans and a tee shirt roughly asked who she was and what she was doing in the area. Before she could reply he reached out to grab her camera which was hanging from her neck. That was a big mistake, she fended off his hand and directed a withering kick to his groin and as he doubled forward clutching it, she delivered a round house kick to the head which put him on the rough dirt road writing in pain. The second man who was without shirt but with a machete in his hand advanced on her. Mistake number two, as he raised his hand with the machete she lunged forward and got in close to him while striking his bicep with so much force from both her arms that the weapon flew out of his grip and landed on the ground. While he was still in a state of shock, she gave him a hip throw rolling him smoothly off her hip and to the ground, she then stomped him in the chest and picked up the machete and with it she gave him a solid slap across his chest that she could see clearly imprinted on his bare skin the words, made in China. She proceeded towards her vehicle leaving them nursing their wounds and wondering what had hit them.

That night while at home reflecting on what had happened earlier in the day and on the direction she was trying to steer her life Juanita was suddenly overwhelmed with a feeling of uncertainty. Could she live up to her vow, would she have the strength to resist the temptation to go back to the old ways. Probably the main reason she questioned herself so much was the fact that what she did was not something that is considered natural, nor was she doing it for the love of it. She was doing it because she felt compelled and driven to conduct that fight against the particular form of evil that had taken from her the most precious part of her life, her family.

It was with all these thoughts haranguing her that she did not have a very restful night.

As if that was not enough, she received a call from Dominic in the DR the very next morning. It was a call to action that was to prove too much for Juanita to resist. After outlining the gist of why he had called Juanita suggested to Dominic that he should take a trip to Jamaica where he could brief her privately and confidentiality.

One week after that call Dominic arrived in Jamaica. He landed at the Montego Bay International airport and from there headed directly to the Holiday Inn hotel in Montego Bay. Juanita joined him later that afternoon and it was a pleasant reunion.

After this initial chit chat, they got down to business, with Dominic laying out all the details.

Dominic explained that there was a Haitian gang that was heavily involved in the drug for guns trade operating between Jamaica and Haiti. But what was more urgent and deplorable about that particular gang was that they were also involved in human trafficking. They not only abducted young Haitian children, especially girls, but they would make incursions across the border into the Dominica Republic where they would also conduct their abductions. The leader of that gang has been identified as Alim Duma.

Alim was well known in Haiti and is reputed to be a very ruthless individual who at an early age was alleged to have murdered his father and older brother one night while they slept.

"So, Dominic, why don't the Haitian police deal with him there in Haiti?"

"Well for one thing he is very popular with most of the people in his area and some of the police are on his payroll." "Secondly he is said to be protected by a voodoo priest and that makes those who are not directly involved with or protecting him keep their distance out of fear."

"I guess belief kills and belief cures as the saying goes." "Well so does Juanita."

"Juanita, we have collected much information on him over the past year but there has never seem to be any urgency in apprehending him or taking him out completely and since he and his gang were more a Haitian problem, we did not show any urgency in getting involved."

"So, what has changed now?"

"Well over the past three months some six young girls have been abducted in the area close to the border between our two countries and the word is out that it is Amin and his gang that are the perpetrators."

"And how did you become involved?"

"My unit has been given the task of dealing with the problem in the shortest possible time, using whatever means."

"And me?"

"Do you want me to spell it out?" "You are my whatever means."

"You seem pretty confident in yourself that I would accept this mission and get involved in something that has the potential to turn quite messy."

"I know it's a long overreach Juanita but after what you experienced with your family and the fact that you would be doing it for your country, I was prepared to take my chance with asking you."

"Dominic, do you realize that my last visit to Dominica Republic was to bring closure to the lifestyle I was living and to turn over a new page." "And here you are pulling me right back in." "It was my sole intention to start living a normal life working on my business and spending time with young people to help them in staying focused in navigating all the twists and turns in this cruel world and to live positive lives."

"Dominic there will be conditions for me accepting this mission."

"Firstly, after this meeting you and I will not meet again until after the mission is completed and that will be if I visit DR on vacation."

"No one else but you must know that I am involved."

"Agreed."

"Well now that we are settled on those conditions, what intelligence have you and your team collected so far?" "Because I am certainly not going in blind or starting from scratch." "It will be a clean in and out mission for me, nothing more than three days."

"Ok, let's go to my room where we will have more privacy and we can have a drink while I fill you in on the details." "By the way my mom doesn't know I am in Jamaica, or she would certainly ask me if I am going to take you back to DR."

"My mom is a trip."

At the end of the meeting, just as Juanita was leaving the room, she turned and hugged Dominic. He returned the hug and held her so tightly that it became emotionally uncomfortable, and she had to break away.

On the drive back home, Juanita went through all that Dominic had said and all the details she had to remember but she also found herself thinking about Dominic for a fleeting moment.

Kareem was waiting at the cottage when she got back home, and he had a meal of Chinese food waiting.

"So where has my errant gypsy been today?" "Have you been chasing after Pancho Villa again or is it the Escobar clan this time?"

Juanita was a bit shocked by the names chosen but she did not show any reaction more than to say.

"No honey nothing as exotic, just a little business trip to Montego Bay."

"Okay, you must be hungry so let us eat as I am famished."

That night Juanita went to bed thinking about Kareem's question. It was a while before she dismissed the thought that he was fishing for information. Juanita knows deep down that if Kareem wanted to check her out, he just had to get onto his friends in the military and that would be done. But for one reason or another he had not, he chose to trust her, and she would do everything to maintain that trust.

Bright and early the day after she had met with Dominic Juanita made a call to Jose in Mexico. She had been thinking of the upcoming mission all night and she wanted to have the resources available when she was ready to make her move.

In the meeting with Dominic, he had told her that Alim almost religiously visited a small bar every Friday and Saturday night for about two hours. From the photos he produced the bar was at the end of a deserted road on the Haitian side of the border just across a gorge. The area around the bar and extending for some distance across the border into the DR was covered with low lying scrub and a few trees on the DR side. It would take a close-up ground reconnaissance to find a suitable spot if she was going to apply her preferred method which would be a sniper's mission as opposed to a close encounter.

Three weeks after speaking to Jose he called to inform Juanita that all was arranged and would be in place once she was in country. She replied that she would be going in the following Wednesday and would be out by Sunday the latest.

Juanita would not leave anything up to chance so just in case Alim did not show up on the Friday night she would be able to take him on the Saturday night.

Juanita arrived in the DR where she picked up a rental vehicle at the airport then booked into a small hotel a few miles from the border with Haiti. She spent the afternoon relaxing by the pool and enjoying the cuisine offered for dinner.

At night fall on Thursday Juanita left the hotel and headed out for her reconnaissance. On the way she picked up Jose and they drove to within a mile of the area of interest. It was now dark, so she got out of the vehicle and began walking on the road for a while then she broke track and went off the road and into the bush where she continued to walk parallel to the road until she was directly across from the bar over on the other side of the gorge. She searched for a suitable place to be used as her hide the following night. Using a hand laser distance measuring device, she recorded a distance of 830 meters. That distance would put the target slightly over the effective range of the rifle which was eight hundred meters. Juanita was confident, however, that she could make the shot.

The weapon of choice for the mission was a SSG 69 bolt action sniper rifle manufactured by Mannlicher. It fires the standard NATO 7.62x51 mm rounds and would be fitted with a top-of-the-line night vision scope.

Having completed her checks Juanita retraced her steps in the woods then emerged to get back into the vehicle. All was set for the following night.

The following day Juanita had a sumptuous breakfast then with a magazine she proceeded to laze by the pool until close to mid-day. She then retired to her room where she spent some time going through details of the mission. She played it over and over in her head until she was quite satisfied. Juanita then listened to music to further get her mind in tune with what was ahead. Her next move was to have an early supper, then dressed in a white long-sleeved shirt and shorts she left the compound in the rental vehicle. She drove around the area for a while stopping at some familiar places from her past.

The evening had now given way to the darkness of the tropical night, so she was on her way. First, she would stop and collect Jose and then be on their way to the target area. On reaching the predetermined spot she stopped the vehicle, collected her weapon, and disappeared into the woods as Jose drove away. By this time Juanita was dressed in black long-sleeved shirt and long black jeans.

She arrived at her chosen spot and began to make herself comfortable for the wait ahead. The wait was not long. Half an hour after she got there the target arrived. She sent the emergency preset text to Jose and hit the send button. The target arrived with two other men. He was a large, towering figure. He wore a beret, perched on top of his huge head and was smoking a large cigar. The short distance from the parking area to the front of the bar was all that Juanita needed. She locked onto him took the first pressure on the trigger and a split second later applied the full pressure and it was all over. As the two men with him looked around in shock and headed into the bar Juanita made her tactical withdrawal. She crouched by the edge of the road and waited for the arrival of Jose. He was there very promptly, and they left the area driving at a moderate speed so as not to attract attention. Once out of the area they stopped, and Juanita let off Jose and changed back into the clothe she left the hotel wearing. Jose would take care of the cleaning up by getting rid of the clothes and anything else that had to be addressed.

The following morning Juanita checked out of the hotel and made her way to the airport. She was then on her way back to Jamaica. Before boarding the aircraft, however, she made one call to Dominic with a rather cryptic message. "Did you receive the present your sister left you?" The reply was "Yes, thanks, love it."

She then dismantled the phone and dropped it in the garbage dumpster.

CHAPTER 15

The day after returning from The Dominica Republic Juanita decided to go to the nearby Oracabessa market to purchase fresh fruits and vegetables. This was more done out of curiosity for what takes place in the market and its environs than out of real need for her to do so. She was accompanied by Karl one of her trusted employees in the boat business. When she entered the market she had no idea she would have been treated like such a celebrity by all the elderly female vendors. Then Karl said to her. "This is what happens when you work with the children in the area and show them such love." "They respect you and pass it on to their parents, so don't be surprised."

"Okay Karl I had no idea my interaction with the children had created such a bond and fan club."

Before Juanita was even finished talking, she caught sight of a familiar face. Although he was turned halfway towards her, there was no doubt mistaking who it was. It was none other than the man whose chest she had tattooed "Made in China" with the machete when she had slapped him with it on their earlier encounter. Juanita could not resist her next move. She walked over to him and tapped him on the shoulder. He turned and on seeing her his eyes took on the look of two miniaturized saucers and his face became somewhat ashen. He turned and fled the market at such speed that all the

82

people around stared with gaping mouth as they wondered his erratic and unreadable action.

"Juanita, what happened to that guy, do you know him?"

"Karl, let's just say he saw his worst nightmare and he couldn't deal with it."

On the way back, after shopping, Juanita explained how she had known the guy and the outcome of the meeting. She jokingly said. "I wonder if he got rid of his tattoo." "I am sure his pride will be hurting long after that slap with the machete." They both laughed as they headed for the jetty. But Karl got in the last word. "Juanita, I think you are a dangerous woman." Then he laughed again.

That afternoon when she shared the story with Kareem, he listened in complete silence then he asked her. "Are you some kind of a lightning rod but instead of attracting lightning you attract trouble?"

"I am not sure where you are going with this, but you could say that." "Trouble or excitement always seem to find me."

"Makes me wonder what happens when you travel overseas and if I should start worrying about your safety."

"No need to my friend I am quite capable of handling myself."

"Okay if you say so my honey, but just think about it." "Two men shot by you in the house after they broke in." "Car chase from Port Antonio." "Shootout on the high seas like James Bond and now attacked by two unknown men." "And those are only the ones I have heard about." "What will it be next honey."

"Fear not my friend I plan to have a long and happy life, and do you want to know the best part, I want to share it with you."

"That's only if you don't give me a heart attack before." "You know what I do and my exposure to danger almost daily, so I am not exactly weak of heart, but I am really concerned about you." "Damned, that is probably what they call love." "No wonder Shakespeare described it this way." "Is love a tender thing?" "It is too rough too rude, too boisterous and it pricks like thorn."

"Wow! You are now seeking peace of mind through Shakespeare, you fascinate me."

"You jest at scars that never felt a wound my dear Juanita."

"Wow! Deep real deep my love." Maybe we should just get some wine and sit here while you quote poetry."

"It's all a joke to you, isn't it?" "Just don't come crying to me when you get hurt."

"So, who should I run too my sweet papi."

"So, I am now papi, why don't you just call me old boy, you little agent provocateur."

"I thought papi sounded sweeter but if you prefer old boy that is what it will be."

She miles, walks over to him and sat on his lap. "You are truly a sweet man you know."

"So where did I go wrong to deserve you?"

They both laugh as he pulled her tight to his chest and wrapped his arms around her.

The next day Juanita was busy with the men mounting two new brackets on one of the boats when the call came. Her day was shattered, but it would get even worst later.

Jose had called to tell her that her police contact in Ciudad Juarez had been murdered by cartel members. He said he would call her later when he had more details.

When Jose called the following day the information he passed on only served to make Juanita go ballistic with anger and strengthen her resolve in continuing the fight against the cartels. She had reached a point where she had been questioning her continuation along that path, but this development had successfully rekindled her desire to continue her crusade regardless of the cost. Juanita learned from Jose that her police friend and two of his coworkers were part of a convoy of three police vehicles that were on the way to intercept a group of vehicles involved in human trafficking. They were ambushed on the way and a fierce gun battle erupted. At the end of it three police were dead, and a number of others were injured the vehicle her friend was in was hit by what appeared to be a handheld rocket launcher. The vehicle was reduced to a smoldering pile of metal. When it was over two of the young girls being trafficked were also killed but the traffickers escaped with the others.

Juanita was incensed by the cruelty of the act and vowed she would retaliate at the soonest possible opportunity. The outcome will not be very pleasant for those involved.

CHAPTER 16

The last bit of information was tantamount to rubbing salt in the wound. Juanita had just been told that Alejandro Quintin the former leader of the Los Fuegos cartel, the same person she had gone to Spain to terminate and had spared his life was the mastermind behind the human trafficking ring. He had quietly established a network stretching from Mexico and other Central American countries through the Caribbean and Europe and all the way to India. Juanita came to the decision that whatever it would cost her, her relationship with Kareem, her business or even her life, she was going after him.

For Juanita to conduct this mission she would have to call upon a number of her trusted sources, and while that was not her preferred way of operating, she realized there was not much choice if she wanted to succeed.

Her first call was to Tom, her DEA friend in Jamaica. Her request was a simple straight forward one; he was to help her in tracking the movements of Alejandro Quintin.

The next call was to Jose, he was to keep a detailed log of the happenings in Mexico as it concerned the cartels and in particular any human trafficking activities, they were involved in. With that and other friendly sources activated it was now a waiting game.

When the time did come it was to present the most ideal opportunity for the intended mission.

Juanita had received word from Tom that Alejandro Quintin was expected be in the Caribbean sometime around the Easter holiday period. The exact location he would be was not yet known but it was expected to be one of the smaller islands in the region.

This information coincided with information received from Jose that the main players in the trafficking network were in the process of planning a trip out to the Caribbean for some kind of a meeting. Those involved were later identified as Julio Martinez and Chris Duggan from Mexico, Alberto Carlos from Colombia, and Pierre Aguilar from Haiti.

It seems the men were to travel separately to the region and would be staying at different islands before coming together for their meeting.

In mid-March it was learnt that the yacht Santa Lucia which is owned by Renaldo Torres a former Commander in the Revolutionary Armed Forces of Colombia (FARC) had been rented by an associate of Julio Martinez. The FARC group was founded in 1964 and was branded as a terrorist organization which fought against the Colombian government. During their period of operation, they were a major player in the narco trafficking business. Although they signed a peace treaty with the government in 2016 and formally dissolved and disbanded, they were not removed from the United States foreign terrorist designation list until November 2021.

The Santa Lucia was rented by Julio Martinez for a trip to the island of Antigua, part of the twin island state of Antigua and Barbuda. The boat was due to be in Antigua during the annual sailing week which is held during the week following Easter.

Sailing week is held at English Harbor, St. Pauls and attracts up to 1500 boats from all over the world and approximately 5,000 visitors and is regarded as one of the top regattas in the world. It is a time of great festivity in Antigua. The streets are crowded with tourists and the nights hum with the sounds of revelry as tourists do what tourists do in tropical islands. There is much music and drinking, with the smell of Antiguan rum permeating the air.

Santa Lucia would dock in English Harbor at the end of a journey that would take it from Colombia to Mexico, on to Venezuela and finally Antigua. It was crewed by an all-Colombian crew, all former members of FARC and very loyal to Renaldo Torres the owner of the boat.

While the boat was headed for Antigua Julio Martinez and Chris Duggan the two Mexicans would fly into Antigua from Miami. Alberto Carlos the Colombian flew to Puerto Rico and then on to Anguilla. Pierre Aguilar the Haitian left his country for St Kitts. All were to remain in place until given the time and date, by Alejandro Quintin, when to move to Antigua where they would join the boat. Alejandro himself was comfortably located at the beautiful Jungle Bay hotel in Dominica. The owner of the hotel had created a farm like environment there. It was replete with tropical plants and fruits of all kinds. Some visitors to the property describe it as the farm that has a hotel on it rather than just a hotel. Little would the very affable, nature loving owner of the hotel know that he was hosting a most vicious and dangerous criminal. He would have been most distraught.

While Alejandro and his band of thugs were busy preparing for their meeting there was someone of a very deadly nature and disposition actively planning their demise.

Juanita on hearing the various bits and pieces had put the puzzle together and was about to launch into action. Once she heard that the boat was on its way to Antigua, she decided to visit her native land of Dominica Republic again. It was to be her staging area for the operation. As usual her cover was that she was there on business, and she did indeed contact persons in the boating business similar to her own.

While Juanita was there in Dominica Republic Jose had arrived in Antigua and was keeping a low profile while keeping a look out for the Santa Lucia.

Juanita finally got word that Alejandro had flown out of Dominica and was headed to Antigua. It was time for Jose to put a critical part of the plan in place. He was to rent a small boat over at Falmouth harbor which is next to English harbor and only separated by a ridgeline, from there the boat would sail into the English harbor at any time without attraction much attention or suspicion. His next move was to sail over to Barbuda where Juanita would join the boat and they would return to Antigua to await the next move by Alejandro. He had by this time also secured the explosive and other equipment that would be needed to complete the mission. On returning to Antigua Juanita remained out of sight on the boat which was now anchored just off the coast at Rendezvous Bay while Jose moved around English Harbor keeping the Santa Lucia under surveillance. That same night when it got sufficiently dark Jose moved the boat to the Western approach to English Harbor just under the foothills of Fort Berkeley. There Juanita slipped unseen into the dark Caribbean water and made her way towards the Santa Lucia. She was clad in a black wetsuit and carried with her a deadly package. She chose her path carefully, trying to avoid the lights as much as possible. All was going well until suddenly she saw a small boat heading directly to her. She took in a deep breath and went deep while at the same time getting out of the path of the speeding boat. It missed her by a few meters, and she returned to her mission. It is at times like these that Juanita appreciated the many hours of training she put in on an almost daily basis to prepare her for the challenges of her risky endeavors.

She reached the boat without any further excitement and affixed the explosive at the point she knew would cause maximum damage through an explosion. She was not worried about collateral damage on this occasion as she had gathered from telephone chatter between Alejandro and his party that the meeting was to take place onboard the boat but outside the harbor. That suited Juanita, perfectly and she would thank Tom for that when she returned home.

The next morning Jose returned the rented boat and went back to keep surveillance on the Santa Lucia. As soon as he saw Alejandro and the others boarding, he would notify Juanita who would at that time be located at the Moondance hotel to the East of English Harbor.

When the call came, Juanita already dressed in hiking gears, immediately got a taxi to drive her up to within a half mile of Shirley Height Lookout which gives a beautiful panoramic view of the harbor and its environs, she continued the rest of the journey on foot. On reaching the Lookout Juanita was awed by the beauty of the harbor below. The water was crystal clear, and it was teeming with all kinds of boats of all description; some were your ordinary pleasure crafts, some fishing boats, and some really majestic yachts. She was proud of herself for deciding not to execute her mission on the Santa Lucia while she was in such a beautiful and serene place.

Shortly after, she saw the Santa Lucia making its way majestically out of the harbor. It was such a pity; she was a beautiful boat. With that Juanita waited a while longer until it had cleared the other boats and the entrance to the harbor then she triggered the bomb. There was a brilliant flash then the accompanying sound of a massive explosion. There was debris and a smoldering fire for a while and then just driftwood. By the time the fireboat and the police arrived there was hardly anything to see.

Juanita made her way down from the lookout and got a taxi back to the hotel where she checked out and headed to the airport for a flight by commuter aircraft to Dominica Republic and the first leg on her journey back home.

On arrival back in Jamaica she was bet at the airport by Kareem. On the way back to the cottage Kareem was not his talkative self and for the most part seemed to be deep in thoughts and as if far away. When they arrived at the cottage, they had an early dinner and then Kareem told her that they needed to talk.

"Juanita, the time has come for you to level with me and clear the air about what you are really up to." "There are just too many strange things happening since we have been seeing each other." Juanita sat and listened in silence. "Do you realize that while you were away two men purporting to be from the United States Coast

Guard visited and boarded your boats claiming that they were conducting security assessment on your operations." "Luckily for you your workers did not buy their story and contacted me after they had left." I immediately contacted our local Coast Guard to find out if they knew anything about such visits." When they told me they had no such knowledge and confirmed that any such occurrence would have been cleared through them I Called the police to do a check on the boats." "Surprise, surprise, they found two very sophisticated bombs one on each boat, set to be activated by remote control hidden on board." "The bombs were removed, and an investigation is underway."

"Juanita there is no doubt in my mind that those bombs were meant for you while you were out at sea." "Have I said enough now to make you understand how unsettling all this is for me?"

"If not on the boat where next will the bomb be placed and will be collateral damage?"

"Kareem, I do understand what you are thinking, and my only reservation is for not leveling with you earlier."

"Juanita, I have known for some time that things were not right, but I somehow wanted to hear it from you." "Well, the time has come, I will not jeopardize my career anymore." "I am a military officer in service of my country and regardless of how you may justify or color your activities in the eyes of my people I would be married to a criminal." "Yes, I said married, because that is what I have been thinking for some time but then things began to happen too fast, and my suspicion escalated." "All those overseas trips and the trail of death that seeded to follow wherever you showed up." "If I could have figured it out who else wont and then what?" "Now it's too late to push back the clock and pretend my reservations are not real."

"Kareem, I will not ask you to change your mind and I will not apologize for what I do but I will say that I admire you a great deal and really wished things could have been otherwise."

"As of tomorrow, I will begin to make arrangements concerning the business and my future endeavors."

"Thank you Juanita and you can rest assured that your secrets are safe with me, and I will always have your back."

With that out of the way they sat mostly in silence on the deck looking out to sea, with a decanter of wine they admired the sunset and watched as the skies filled with the beauty of the heavenly bodies.

Later they retired and made love with a passion that could only be eclipsed by the first time they had done so all the way over in Western Canada.

Juanita was true to her words and the following day she began deciding how best to dispose of her business. In thinking about the boats, she thought of the crew who had worked so faithfully and loyally with her. It was then that she decided to approach Kareem about taking over the business with the one condition that he maintained the staff.

Kareem agreed to the deal and the necessary documents were prepared in order to transfer ownership. It was very necessary for this to be done so as to clear her involvement and eliminate any possible targeting of Kareem by any who might come after her. At the same time, it gave her the freedom to continue her quest, because rest assured, she would be popping up again somewhere in the future to take care of business the only way she knows.

CHAPTER 17

On leaving Jamaica Juanita headed for her native Dominica Republic, there she spent two weeks before heading off for Vancouver Island in Canada. She rented a cottage with the intention of spending about six months there. Initially she was a bit restless and forlorn as she began to have flashbacks of her meeting with Kareem there and the start of their romantic involvement. She, however, did not allow her feelings and memories to detract her from her main reason for being there. She had come to relax and reflect as she slowed down the pace of her life, which at times she thought was certainly spinning out of control.

While there she kept up with the news from around the world and read anything she could get her hands on. In addition, she maintained her fitness program and visited parks and places of relaxation. In the process she became an avid kayaker, and many days would find her on a nearby lake paddling away to the sound of music from her mobile phone. Soon the outside world as she knew it was becoming a blur as she wrapped herself in the tranquility of her pristine environment and her present lifestyle.

One afternoon while relaxing by the fireplace Juanita started flipping through a copy of a National Geographic magazine, she caught sight of an article about the Amazon region of Brazil. She was particularly intrigued by Indigenous tribes known as the uncontacted because they lived in isolation in villages in the dense jungle and did not venture out into the developed areas. She was also struck by pictures and stories of its unique flora and fauna. In a heartbeat Juanita was ready to go there to explore for herself.

Having made up her mind Juanita suddenly remembered that she had promised her friend from the Dominica Republic that she wanted the two of them to go exploring all the small Caribbean islands. She had said she wanted to get an intimate and thorough idea of the pulse and lifestyle of the various islands.

She would not disappoint Dominic, so the trip to Brazil would be scheduled for after her Caribbean exploits.

Before departing Canada, Juanita used the opportunity to purchase some top-of-the-line camera equipment. The plan was to use them extensively on her Caribbean trip so as to master their features and capabilities before going to Brazil.

When Juanita arrived back in Dominica Republic, Dominic was overjoyed and demonstrated all the characteristics of a doting schoolboy. They were both extremely happy to see each other and there was no hiding it.

At the end of the three-week spent visiting the islands of St. Lucia, St Vincent, Grenada, and Dominica it was time to head home. But the final evening of their trip was a defining moment in the character of the two individuals.

While sitting at the poolside at the Jungle Bay Hotel they sipped wine and looked out to sea in the direction of the land formation known as Scotts Head. Dominic was lost in his own world, thinking of the wonderful time they had spent together and where it could be heading. Juanita on the other hand was already shutting down any feelings of emotion. She had enjoyed the break and all that happened, but she was now ready to close the chapter and move on. Out of respect for Dominic's feeling, however, she would gently ease out of the situation without causing him too much pain. After a late dinner and a night of extreme passion it was time to depart for Dominica Republic by way of Antigua.

Juanita kept a low profile for the next week, only visiting with Dominic and his mother once and for the rest of the time kept herself busy in her hotel room and between the gym and the beach. At the end of the week she left, telling Dominic that she was heading to Miami. Juanita had returned to being as cold as the snow she had left behind in Canada a few weeks ago. She was again the lone warrior, unfettered and extremely dangerous.

Miami, however, was only a quick stop on the way to Guyana in South America. Juanita spent two days in Guyana visiting the Kaieteur Falls high up on the Potaro River and exploring the capital Georgetown. The falls was majestic and breathtaking and Georgetown in its rustic beauty and colonial architecture was interesting and intriguing.

The trip from Georgetown to Bogota was a long one over very mountainous terrain which created much turbulence even at the high altitude the aircraft flew. Some passengers were visibly shaken at times, but Juanita maintained her composure and even helped in comforting two children who sat next to her.

Juanita spent one night in Bogota and then left by air for Leticia.

Leticia is the southernmost city in the Republic of Colombia, located in the area known as Tres Fronteras because that is the area where the countries of Colombia, Brazil and Peru come together. It is one of the major ports on the Amazon River. It serves as Colombia's shipping point for tropical fish for the aquarium trade.

When the long-standing border dispute between Colombia and Peru, which involved Leticia, was ended in 1934 by the League of Nations a significant change was made to the population of Leticia. The Colombian government remained wary of the Peruvians and decided to populate Leticia with people from Bogotá in order to ensure that the town remained loyal to Colombia. Most of the people who came from Bogotá during that period still live in Leticia. Since that time Leticia has expanded significantly, however, the city's industries have not changed much and agriculture and tourism are still the main sources of income. In fact, tourism has developed to the extent that it is a recognized international tourist site, attracting both international students and visitors to study and enjoy the attractions of surrounding areas and as Juanita would find out it also became a hub for drug smuggling from Colombia to Brazil.

On arriving in Leticia Juanita headed out by boat to her final destination in the Javari Valley. On the way she passed the town of Tabatinga located on the Western edge of Amazonas

The population of Tabatinga municipality is quite heterogeneous. It is formed by Brazilians, Peruvians, Colombians, and Indigenous people of different ethnic groups.

The city's economy is built around an informal economy and subsistence agriculture. There is also a significant number of public sector jobs generating extensive financial exchange in the Colombian city of Leticia. This knowledge was not wasted on Juanita as she now began to see Leticia for what it was, a significant player in criminal activities.

Because of its extensive border with Colombia and Peru, Tabatinga is regarded by the Federal Police and the Brazilian Army as one of the main points of entry for cocaine into Brazil, for that reason and because it is a major Brazilian city a large number of federal police officers, federal revenue agents and federal prosecutors, are located there. It was another reason, Juanita avoided staying there choosing instead to stay in the Javari Valley area, the other reason was that she wanted to be as close as possible to the Indigenous population and the exotic flora and fauna of the region.

The Javari Valley is one of the largest indigenous territories in Brazil, encompassing an area larger than the country of Austria. It is named after the Javari River, the most important river of the region, and which since 1851 forms the border with Peru.

The Brazilian government has made it illegal for non-Indigenous people to enter the territory. In order to monitor activities in the region the government utilizes aircraft.

The Javari Valley is home to some 3,000 indigenous peoples of Brazil. These groups have varying levels of contact with the outside world. The truly uncontacted indigenous peoples are estimated to be more than 2,000 individuals belonging to at least fourteen tribes. They live deep inside its reservation areas in nineteen known villages that were identified from the air. That makes it the greatest concentration of isolated groups in the Amazon and the world.

Juanita stayed at the Castro Alves hotel in Atalaia do Norte in the Javari Valley reserve. The distance from Atalaia do Norte to Leticia is approximately nineteen (19) miles as the crow flies and forty-six point five (46.5) miles by river which is the main means of transport between the two towns.

The day after checking into her hotel Juanita was on the move, armed only with her cameras and much confidence. She, however, did not throw caution to the wind and made sure she checked out the safety of the area and any potential dangers she should be aware of as she moved around.

Feeling confident with the overall security situation her next move was to contact a boatman who would be able to take her to places along the river where she could get her photos and also to link her with others who could take her into the forest for a closer look at the wildlife that could be seen and photographed.

During the next few days, she made a number of excursions into the jungle, being careful not to venture into the prohibited areas. She also made a number of trips up to Tabatinga and Leticia. She particularly enjoyed the trips to Leticia as she got a chance to visit some of the regular tourist attractions and to converse with the population from a variety of ethnic groups. While enjoying all the positive elements of these trips she became acutely cognizant of the fact that there were a number of underlying issues creating some tension. Some of these issues involved the drug trade in the area while some involved the incursions by outsiders into the protected indigenous areas.

These groups would enter the area to hunt and capture or kill wildlife such as alligators, turtles, exotic birds and a variety of other rare animals and fish including the arapaima which is one of the largest freshwater fish in the world and has a long history of commercial hunting and exploitation. These incursions were very frustrating to the uncontacted indigenous peoples, who now felt that the government was not doing enough to protect their lifestyle and livelihood.

On one of her canoe trips Juanita overheard that the headman of the Isolados do Sao Jose, indigenous village had called a meeting with all the headmen from the other villages to discuss the matter and to formulate plans to deal with the intruders. The matter had become even more urgent as it had been rumored that the intruders were in the process of recruiting a hitman in Bogota to take out one or two of the headmen so as to send a message to the other villages who want to obstruct them in their operations in the protected zone.

Juanita listened with detached interest, but on reaching her hotel that evening she could not help but reflecting on the issue. She saw it as a David and Goliath issue, and it began to get under her skin. She started to formulate a plan.

Juanita soon realized that this would probably be her most daring and audacious mission if she decided to go through with it. Maybe it was all of these that rather than deterring her were egging her on. She would first have to discretely meet with the headman of the Isolados do Sao Jose, indigenous village, then she would need to learn all she could about the potential hit man next she would need to get the necessary gears and equipment to execute the mission. Juanita also realized that time was of the essence and so she had to move fast in order to prevent the impending murders of the headmen.

The following day while out with her, now personal, boatman she concocted a story in order to get into the Sao Jose village. She asked him if he could arrange for her to meet the headman of the area as she would like to talk to him about permission to go into his area for the purpose of getting pictures of some special plants that she learnt exist there. Juanita's real reason for wanting to get into the area was actually to conduct an on the ground reconnaissance of the area. She needed to know the trails in and out and the nature of the land formation and quality. The last thing she wanted was to end up in some sticky swamp that does not exist on the maps of the area, especially since she more than likely would be operating at night.

Two days later Juanita got a response from the head man who agreed to meet her discretely in the town of Benjamin Constant which is about halfway between the town she was staying and the town of Tabatinga. As soon as they had privacy and the formalities were over Juanita got straight to the point. "I understand you are having some problems with persons entering into your region and carrying out illegal activities, it that a fact?" The headman hesitated for a moment, so Juanita continued. "I understand that they are now threatening to kill you and another headman to send a message not to hinder them operating in your area, is that a fact?" The headman nodded in the affirmative. "In that case listen carefully to my next question." "Would you like to get rid of this threat?"

"Yes, we would but we don't know where to turn as my people don't have the experience or resources to deal with it and the government doesn't seem to be interested."

"Suppose I tell you that I know where I can get help for you would you be interested?"

"Yes, we would be interested as it's the livelihood of our people that is at stake."

"Do you understand that the hit men might have to be eliminated?" "Without any implications for your people, of course."

"Yes, I understand."

"Very good, for that reason we will not meet like this again, and you are to say nothing to anyone, not even the other headmen."

"So, what do I do now?"

"Nothing, just know that you have a friend and that something will happen soon to those who are threatening to cause you and your people harm."

Juanita is convinced that after the meeting the headman would not be able to recognize her again as she was heavily disguised, wearing a native dress, a bandana and two long plaits of hair similar to the hair of the natives of the region. She also wore large earrings and native jewelry.

True to her words Juanita did not meet with the headman again but exactly ten days after meeting with him she found herself settling into her chosen sniper's hide, on a dark moonless night.

The hide was along the main trail used by the poachers who entered the area and lead to the village of Sao Jose. Covered in her camouflage netting and other paraphernalia she had to make herself as comfortable as possible as she would be there until night fall of the following night, which is the time her targets were expected to make their move on the village. The hide was sufficiently large that she was not cramped in it, but she had taken all precautions to conceal it from the air as well as anyone wandering nearby. She had taken the added precaution of spraying the immediate surroundings with animal and insect repellants.

Now all she had to do was wait for the hitmen, Tata Vasquez, to come into her line of fire in her chosen kill zone.

The night passed slowly except for one brief moment when two shadowy figures decided that the area of her kill zone was an ideal place to have a romantic episode and so they did and just as quietly as they came, they disappeared into the darkness of the night. Juanita could not help but smile.

The following day came with all the heat and humidity of a tropical jungle, but Juanita was prepared for it. She had planned well and the supplies she had solicited from her sources were perfect for the conditions.

Due to the denseness of the jungle the transition from day to night is rather short and so as the sun began to go down Juanita must have had a flash back to her Marine training, when on field exercises daybreak and sunset were drilled into the mind as periods of maximum alert or "Stand To" as it was called.

Juanita was now on full alert.

In front of the party of the hitman was one man who appeared to be one of the natives of the region. He was short in statue and carried a red bag slung over his shoulder, he moved furtively along the track as if expecting something to happen. He, however, had nothing to fear although he was inadvertently playing a crucial role in the impending demise of the other man following close behind. The bag he had slung over his shoulder was the key. Knowing that there would be limited light Juanita had to make sure she did not make a mistake with the target and kill some unsuspecting member of the village. The escort, therefore, was unknowingly identifying the target by the bag he carried.

Juanita was comfortable, her breathing was controlled and even as she took the first pressure of the trigger then second and the baseball cap flew from the head of the man in her sight as the head exploded from the impact of her bullet, she chambered another round and fired again into the body as it crumbled to the ground. Suddenly there was the unmistakable crack of a rifle from down the trail and impact of a bullet in a tree stump next to her. She quickly rolled to her left and took cover behind the stump that had been hit, then two more rounds rang out. It dawned on her that there was a second hitman in the party, she had to think fast how to deal with this new development. Juanita then fired one round in the direction the shot came from and again rolled to a new position while keeping as close to the ground as possible. The native had by this time disappeared like a bat out of hell, ditching his bag as he ran. Making use of her night scope Juanita soon located the shooter. He was lying prone at the base of a large tree. Taking a calculated risk Juanita got up and made a quick dash in a direction heading from the trail and using the trees as cover. One shot rang out, but she kept going then she went to ground. She waited for a while, then just as she suspected the gunman broke cover and headed in the direction she had run. She watched him as he cautiously moved forward. Not wanting to lose her the hitman speeded up his steps and soon passed the position where she was hiding. Juanita was now behind him; the hunter had become the hunted. Juanita had no intention of prolonging the encounter, so she carefully aimed and brought him down with a well-aimed shot, followed by another.

Juanita returned to her hide and quickly gathered all her covering into one camouflage bag and headed into the darkness of the jungle along a path she had mapped out beforehand. The path took her to the edge of one of the small streams where at a predetermined spot she sank the bag with its content into the water.

The next morning when her boatman called for her, she was on spot, armed with her cameras and ready for her photo shoots. He did not mention anything about the shooting.

Juanita spent two more days in the area doing her usual visits to the regular tourist's spots and doing her photo shoots.

On the last day of her stay, and on her way to the airport, she gave her boatman a substantial tip and a framed photo of one of the flowers in the area to be delivered to the headman with the simple message thanks, from a friend.

Juanita was on the move again, overnighting in Bogota and then on to Miami where she planned to stay for a prolonged period to again readjust and reflect.

On arriving in Miami, she bought a new phone and made three calls; first to Jose to let him know she was safe, then she called Dominic and lastly Kareem. After the calls she planned to make an all-out effort to live as normal a life as possible, until she had to move again.

EPILOGUE

Juanita is free spirited, and mission driven by her passion for justice. She sometimes thinks of what it would be to live, what most consider, a normal life. She was once on the way to doing that, but all her plans were upended by the tragic murder of her family and from that day on she has been charting her own path in the pursuit of justice or what others might see simply as revenge.

Printed in the United States
by Baker & Taylor Publisher Services